STAR
SURVIVOR

VERONICA SCOTT

*To my daughters Valerie and Elizabeth, my brother David and my best
friend Daniel
To Michael R for all his encouragement and love of the Sectors!*

Acknowledgments

Julie C and The E-book Formatting Fairies!

CHAPTER ONE

She'd known it was a mistake to agree to venture out of her cabin, much less to go to the casino, but her companions had been begging her to join them on this final night of the cruise. A woman couldn't concentrate on business all the time, could she? Not even to avoid unpleasant realities. A migraine nagged above her eye, threatening to become full blown, and the loud thumping music in the casino aggravated the pain. Twilka Zabour paused at the entrance to the private, high stakes gaming area and froze.

Oh, yes, a major flashback was inevitable now. Not just because the lights and the music and the crowd were reminding her so forcibly of the last night on board the *Nebula Dream*, but because of the man standing in the center of a largely female, laughing group of passengers. He stood with his back to her, thank the lords, and all she could see were his broad shoulders and that glossy, unbound mane of hair, but the high roller running the table was a D'nvannae Brother.

Khevan.

The memories were a physical pain in her gut as the room spun around her.

"Drink. I need a drink," she said, grabbing at the glasses balanced on the tray of a passing server. She didn't care what they were, nor was she displeased to find the goblets contained two completely different feelgoods. Even as the waiter exclaimed in annoyance and her own companions exchanged astonished glances, she shoved the now empty glasses at the man, snatched a third from his tray, swirls of orange and green froth, and sauntered forward. Twilka headed to the table with a casualness she in no way felt, her nerves taut as a bowstring, her pulse pounding. The migraine took hold with a vengeance now, fueled by tension and the feelgoods. At least she'd worn a killer dress.

"Twenty thousand on the red," she said, having seen his bet and choosing the opposite. "I'll spin." Sipping the abominable, too sweet concoction, she leaned over to spin the retro wheel, giving the room a full view of her cleavage, accented with perfume dust and temporary diamond-studded tattoos.

There was a growing silence around the table. She didn't think the onlookers knew who he was—had been—to her. *She* was famous, her face appearing every-where as the embodiment of her brand, but he was just a D'nvannae. In reality, Khevan could never be dismissed as "just" anything, could he? Her companions had caught up to her, Lissa and Jord standing at her side, slightly behind. Tossing her hair, she raised her glass as the croupier proclaimed her win. "Again." She leaned over and licked Jord's ear, caressing the outline with her tongue as sensuously as she could manage in her highly fraught state of mind. She'd taken him by surprise, but he played along, putting his arm around her waist and pulling her close, turning so her hip curved into his crotch, spilling the drink a bit as he nuzzled her neck.

"The lady wins again," said the dealer.

"Your lucky night," Khevan said, inclining his head to her slightly.

Lords, his voice was as deep and sensuous as ever. Twilka grabbed the table rail with her free hand. Did he know who she was? Of course he did, but the bastard was pretending not to recognize her. "Available for contract, I see."

"Technically true, but traveling to an outlying temple for a required ritual," he said. His handsome, tattooed face gave nothing away. "There would have to be an emergency for me to take a contract tonight."

"Did you want to let the bet ride?" asked the croupier.

"No," she said abruptly. "I don't tempt fate too far any more. Cash me out." Sick of the game, barely able to see for the lightning flashes in her field of vision caused by the migraine, she abandoned her drink and took Jord's arm. "I think we've wasted enough time here, don't you?" Beaming at Lissa, she added, "Let's go to the cabin and start the party again."

She stumbled ever so slightly as she spun around. Jord kept her upright and they walked away. "What the seven hells were you doing?" he asked in a low voice. "Did you know that guy?"

"It was him, wasn't it?" High pitched and excited, Lissa's tone betrayed her fascination. "Your D'nvannae?"

"Not mine, never mine," she said, biting her lip as too much of the truth slipped out. Fearing he was watching her, dreading that he wasn't, she kept walking until she'd put enough distance between herself and the high stakes area not to be seen. Then she stopped abruptly, pulling her arm away from Jord's grip. "Listen, I don't want to ruin your evening. You've both worked hard this trip. I'm going to my cabin, but I want you to stay and enjoy the last night of the cruise." She fumbled for the credit chip. "Take this; win or lose, I don't care, but have fun. See you in the morning."

"Are you sure, boss?" Jord took the chip.

"I'm positive." She straightened her spine and made a shooing motion. "Go, have fun. You know we'll be working 24/7 once we reach the planet tomorrow."

"Are you sure you're okay?" Lissa hesitated. "You're pale."

"I knew I needed more makeup." She forced herself to laugh.

Jord pretended to bite the edge of the credit chip. "Pure gold. Come on, Liss, the boss wants us to party, and I, for one, am ready."

Her personal assistant chewed her lip, a dubious expression on her face, but allowed herself to be drawn away. Twilka gave them an airy wave and walked out of the casino. She forced herself to go a few feet down the corridor and then had to lean on the wall with one hand, as the combined feelgoods and the migraine threatened to topple her. Rubbing her stomach with her free hand, she took a deep breath.

"Do you need help, Miss Zabour?"

The person intruding on her privacy was the ship's security guy; what was his name? Red?

"No, I'm fine, had to catch my breath for a moment," she lied with practiced ease.

He stepped away for a moment to grab a chair from the café close by and returned to guide her into it. "Sickbay is on this level if you're unwell. I'm sure Dr. Shane…"

"I said, I'm fine. A bit dizzy is all, nothing to concern you. Headache. I have meds in my cabin."

"I'll be happy to escort Miss Zabour to her cabin."

She closed her eyes to keep from crying. His voice was exactly the same as it'd been all those years ago, deep, rich with promise. Why had he followed her? She couldn't let him see her weak. Exerting her last ounce of willpower, Twilka rose and managed not to throw up. "I don't require assistance from either of you." She walked off.

Passing the passenger gravlift with a shudder, she paused at the top of the sweeping retro staircase to center her balance.

"Still not a fan of modern antigrav, I see."

She felt his breath on her neck and the bulk of his presence right behind her. "Some things never change. Other things you can't count on at all, can you?" Twilka began the descent, moving carefully. Her damn shoes were pieces of art, but not practical. Ironic if she broke her neck now, here. "I don't need your help—you can go delight your admirers."

Her ankle twisted and only his iron grip on her arm kept her from tumbling the rest of the way to the next deck and fulfilling her own prophecy. "You used to be able to handle your feelgoods," he said, as he escorted her down the stairs. "Time to cut back maybe?"

"What the fuck do you care?" At the bottom, she wrenched her arm free, knowing he allowed her to go. No one could break a D'nvannae's hold unless he permitted it. "I'll say this one more time, I don't need your help and I don't want you near me." She moved as fast as she could toward her cabin, wanting this encounter with her past to be over.

But he stayed with her, adjusting his stride to hers. "We should take this quirk of fate bringing us together and talk."

"Is that what you think this is, fate? I call it a nightmare and we have nothing to talk about. You left me. Went running back to your flaming bitch Lady…" She bit her lip so hard she tasted blood. She was not doing this with him. She'd never give him another chance to destroy her.

"Twilka, it wasn't as simple as it appeared when we first escaped the *Nebula Dream*. Please."

"No." She saw people staring and realized she must have shouted. She'd arrived at her cabin and she had no intention of permitting him inside. She faced him, noting his restored full face tattoo, the scarlet *tariqna* curling over his high cheekbones and strong brow, proclaiming his rank in the service of the Red Lady. "First the bitch tries to kill you—tries to incinerate me—and then she welcomes you with open arms? How much did you crawl? What did she make you do?" She held up one hand as he parted his lips to answer her. "Forget I asked. I don't really give a damn about the details of how you got reinstated. Did you know I waited for a week? Not that you cared." The rush of anger-fueled adrenaline was better than any feelgood high. She abandoned any attempt at self-control. *All right, let's have this out here and now, and staring bystanders be damned.* "You didn't even have the courtesy to say goodbye. To send a message. Nothing. After all we'd shared, after the promises we made to each other. Finally, the White Lady's monks came to tell me I should leave, threw me out of her monastery, oh, so politely, escorted me to my father's ship, and sent me home. I guess I wasn't anything more than a Brotherhood groupie to you. A Socialite novelty fuck."

"You were always more to me, much more."

He touched her cheek and she averted her face to keep herself from falling into his arms. Another reason not to allow him into her cabin. "Apparently not. Now, leave me alone or I'll complain to ship's security. Even a D'nvannae can be thrown in the brig for a few hours." She heard the portal to her cabin slide open and took a step toward the open door. He was silent. She risked one final glance at him and saw him standing there, face a blank mask to hide whatever he was thinking. She almost wavered, but then she scooted inside the cabin, door sliding shut to cut off her view of him.

With a scream of frustration, she threw her expensive purse across the room, tore off her shoes and hurled them at the far bulkhead, then staggered barefoot into the bedroom, falling onto the bed weeping, whether in grief or anger or both, she couldn't say. "Ship, I need headclear and migraine med, now." She got the request out in between gasping sobs.

Efficiently, the AI delivered the requested injects to the bedside stand. Not looking, Twilka gave herself first one, then the other, and curled up in a ball, heedless of her expensive dress.

"Do you require the doctor's attention?" the ship asked.

"I'm fine." Rolling onto her back, she relaxed as the meds kicked in, erasing the feelgoods' poison and the violent effects of the migraine. "Is he gone?"

"The D'nvannae Brother has re-entered the casino on Level A."

Good. Because if he'd still been out there, she might have given in to the temptation to talk to him. And conversation would have led to…other things. "Nothing further is required, Ship."

"Have a good evening, Passenger Zabour." The AI ganglion turned itself off with a click.

Rising to shed the ruined dress and go wash her face, Twilka reflected wearily on the irony of meeting him again here, on a cruise ship. *I used to dream of finding him, of making him tell me what happened, trying to change his mind, and now I don't care. Absolutely no use rehashing the past. Not the good moments or the crushing ones. Too painful.* "I guess I grew up a lot in the last few years, despite myself," she said out loud. Pulling on a silky black nightgown, she removed the rest of her skillfully applied makeup and combed her hair into submission.

Because she wanted to share her unsettled emotions with someone and there was a severely limited subset of people who understood the full story, she sent a quick vidmessage to her friend Mara Jameson. *You'll never guess who I ran into tonight—the Brother himself, as cryptic as ever. Hugs.* Mara would get it, would fill in all the subtext of confusion and other emotions battering Twilka. Mara excelled at reading between the lines.

Climbing onto the bed again, she gathered all the pillows and reclined against them. Extending her palms, cupped, she closed her eyes for a moment, visualizing the White Lady's peaceful garden on Temple Home, as she often did nowadays to center herself when she needed a calm respite from her hectic life. When she reopened them, a pale white tariqna coiled in the air above her hands, wings spread as if ready for flight. Tiny, maybe only three inches high, the creature seemed so real, so alive, yet didn't move or make a sound. Baleful glowing blue eyes stared into hers.

She clapped her hands to make it disappear and laid back. It had been years since she'd let herself summon the apparition, a remnant of her experiences toward the end of their nightmare escape from the dying *Nebula Dream*. With awe, the White Lady's priests said it was a rare sign of her special favor, but couldn't explain what it was good for or why Twilka now possessed the ability to summon the tiny beast.

Some kind of pretty but useless parlor trick. A souvenir, a consolation prize.

She hurled an inoffensive pillow at the bulkhead before closing her eyes. She and Khevan had been promised a meeting with the White Lady herself, but then he'd been lured into seeing his Red Lady one final time and never returned.

Hot tears started again and Twilka rolled onto her side, burrowing into the remaining pillows. *I'm never going to be over this, not if I live to be three hundred. People think we survived the wreck when so many others died, and we should be grateful and never complain, never look back. They have no idea how the trauma lingers. It was a mistake to agree to travel on this ship without going into cryo sleep like I usually do for these business trips.* Heart aching, she felt herself slipping into sleep and prayed she wouldn't have the nightmares tonight.

CHAPTER TWO

Khevan accepted his red and black leather bag from the *Nebula Zephyr* steward, tipped the man a credit, and left the shuttle. He'd been braced to encounter Twilka again this morning, half hoping, half dreading another chance to talk to her, but she and her party weren't aboard the little ship. Maybe this planet wasn't her final destination. He walked through the passenger arrival area of the busy spaceport and cleared the bureaucracy easily, since D'nvannae weren't subject to most regulations, per the treaty between the Sectors and the Red Lady.

Two lay brothers were waiting for him, easy to spot in their scarlet robes. One took his bag as the other welcomed him to the planet. "We're honored to have you here to conduct training and give the blessing at the ritual next week," the man said deferentially. "The flitter is this way."

Not feeling honored, Khevan walked with them in the direction indicated. He had no idea why his orders had been changed to send him here. He enjoyed teaching the younger brothers specialized martial arts classes, but what was so urgent he had to be pulled off his assignment with the big Grunmark archaeological dig at a promising Ancient Observer site, he had no idea. There'd been vague language in the orders about assessing the chief brother at this planet's temple, but a cursory check into the records told him this outpost was audited not long ago, top to bottom. The installation made credits above the required minimum, it had plenty of new recruits, and appeared to be totally dedicated to the will of the Red Lady. All was in order.

But no one questioned the Lady's whims, least of all him. Not anymore. He'd learned his lesson. Hadn't he?

At least he'd seen Twilka, even if it had taken the entire voyage to manage a few moments alone with her. Unsatisfactory moments. He unclenched his fists and ran through a brief mental exercise to clear his head before anyone noticed the tension in his frame. What had he expected, after all? And what if she had been welcoming, willing to forgive? He, of all men, knew what disaster lay in that direction. No, the outcome was vastly better this way than the fulfillment of any forlorn hopes he might have harbored for five years.

Seeking to divert his thoughts as they flew over the city to reach the temple, which occupied a massive plateau on the outskirts, he asked, "Where's the White Lady's temple located?" There was no mistaking the dramatic façade of his own Lady's edifice, which would be visible from virtually anywhere in the city. Flamboyance was one of the Red Lady's cherished hallmarks.

The pilot gave him a surprised glance, but answered readily enough. "Beside the river, in a garden complex."

Interesting. Usually the two complexes were close together, as if to give a person a chance to decide easily between them. *Or as if to allow one sister to keep an eye on the other's plots and machinations.* Of course, he had no business with the White Lady. He wondered if Twilka had ever talked to her, after he was reabsorbed into the fold of the Red Lady's adherents.

"We'll be landing in five minutes," said the brother.

Annoyed with himself for becoming distracted with contemplation of his unresolved relationship with Twilka Zabour, who was nothing to him now, after all, he leaned forward and began asking penetrating questions about the training program at this monastery.

The place was as efficiently run as the audit results he'd perused indicated. He was given a large, luxurious set of rooms as befit his high rank and personal ties to the Lady herself. He spent the afternoon teaching an advanced class and was pleased at their level of knowledge and eagerness to learn. He endured a long, boring dinner with the Chief Monk, who was understandably hostile in an extremely polite way. The Lady liked to play her senior brothers against each other—the politics of their order were intricate and deadly.

After dinner, there was entertainment, and finally Khevan was free to excuse himself and take refuge in the rooms he'd been assigned. Changing out of his formal all black, all leather uniform into a flowing robe, he wandered onto the balcony overlooking the city and caught himself wondering where Twilka might be at this moment.

A knock at the door interrupted his train of thought. Frowning, he went to open it, ready to blast whoever dared disturb him at this hour. He'd taken pains at dinner to be clear he wanted no company, no member of the Sisterhood to share his bed. The angry words died on his lips as he beheld the Chief Brother himself.

"Apologies for intruding on your private meditations, Brother Khevan, but this was just delivered for you." He motioned to a lay brother standing by his side and the man extended a golden tray bearing a gleaming puzzle box made of red jade, intricate carvings on all sides.

He stared at the container for a moment, fury gathering. How dare they try to command him when he was in their temple on a specific errand for the Red Lady? When he outranked every person here, including the man facing him? Jaw clenched, he said, "I'm not here to take a contract."

"And, of course, if the commission was for my own temple, I'd be assigning one of my own brothers," the monk said smoothly. "I have a well-honed cadre, capable of any assignment. This was sent for you specifically, under the seal of Temple Home."

Something important then. Impossible to refuse. Khevan plucked the box from the tray with a casualness he had to work hard to maintain. "Well then, I have no argument. Thank you." He'd be damned if he was going to open it in front of the lower ranking brothers. "Is there anything else?"

The lay brother clearly wished himself elsewhere. The Chief Monk was made of sterner stuff. Eyes glittering as he took a final glance at the box, he bowed fractionally. "Not at the moment. My temple stands ready to assist in any way you may require."

Khevan acknowledged the offer with a slight nod and shut the door absently, rotating the puzzle box in his long fingers. *Cold day in the seven hells when I ask for help from any in the Order.* He walked to the bed, sat on the plush satin cover, and rapidly worked the mechanism. The Red Lady relished her rituals, her mysteries, and the archaic method of transmitting a special contract pleased her. Noiselessly, the lid rose to reveal a small square of parchment nestled on the cushioned red interior. The scarlet symbol for assassination glowed, written in what he'd been told was her own people's language, now long dead and vanished. All members of the Brotherhood recognized it on sight, however, as well as the one for safeguarding life, which was their other, less utilized specialty. Every assignment and all contracts ultimately depended on Her whim. He plucked the paper from the box and unfolded the message, seeking the name of the one he was to hunt down and kill.

Twilka Zabour.

The dreams she couldn't escape for long were especially bad tonight. Twilka tossed and turned on the huge bed in the city's most luxurious hotel, more than a little afraid to seek more sleep. She'd clawed her way out of the nightmare where she was surrounded by laughing, faceless drunks, intent on living their last few hours of life aboard the *Nebula Dream* by passing her around among themselves. In the dream, there was no help coming, no rescue, and she woke screaming. Heart pounding, she lay still for a moment before reaching for the glass of water at the bedside. Should she take the meds her doctor had given her to suppress the memories?

No, the prescription stuff made her into a robot who'd sleepwalk through tomorrow's activities, and she needed all her wits about her in the negotiations. Taking the glass, she kicked her way free of the covers and strolled barefoot to the private terrace, high above the planet's surface. Inhaling a deep breath of the flower-scented air, she took one tentative step onto the balcony, clutching the door handle with her free hand. Acrophobia was a bitch. As she sipped the water, she reflected on the irony that she, of all people, was reluctant to take a drug to quell the nightmares. "A legal one no less," she muttered to herself. *After years of enjoying all the feelgoods all the time with no regard for consequences.*

The view of the city was breathtaking, all colorful twinkly lights at this hour. Raising her eyes to the plateau, she took a deep breath. The Red Lady's oversize temple dominated the horizon, glowing ruby like a baleful eye. Shivering, wishing she'd put on her robe, Twilka pivoted to re-enter the room. With a stifled scream, she saw a dark shadow standing beside the bed. Breaking the water glass on the door frame and holding the jagged base fragment as a weapon, she said, "I've activated my personal panic button. The hotel's security detail will be here in a minute. Leave now and I won't press charges."

He stepped into the moonlight. "We need to talk. Cancel the alarm."

Khevan. She sagged against the balcony door, allowing the broken glass to roll from her hand onto the carpet. "I told you, we have nothing left to discuss. Anything between us died a long time ago."

There was pounding on the door. "Miss Zabour?"

He didn't even glance at the portal, intent on her. "Send them away."

"The hotel has orders to check on me in person if the alarm is triggered."

"Make it fast." There was a flicker and she couldn't see him any longer. If she squinted, the air shimmered with a faint distortion where he'd been.

Another D'nvannae trick. Giving the spot where he presumably stood a wide berth, she went to the door and opened it. Blaster in hand, the security chief scanned the room behind her. "Are you all right, Miss Zabour?"

"I'm fine. I had a nightmare and I was confused when I first awakened." She lied with ease. There had been such incidents before.

"I'll have to check the room."

Stepping aside, she invited him to enter with a wave of her hand. "I broke my water glass, so watch out for the fragments."

"I'll have housekeeping send a robo to clean up the mess," he said, moving through her suite with efficient speed. He scanned every possible spot a person could hide.

"In the morning will be fine. I need my sleep." Twilka forced herself to fake an elaborate yawn.

The second man remained outside in the hall while his team lead finished the quick search of the room, closets included. Twilka stood by silently, occasionally glancing at the minor visual distortion where Khevan lurked. "Thank you for answering so promptly," she said, as she escorted the officer to the door. For a moment, she was tempted to step outside with him and escape the conversation Khevan was determined to have, but she was angry he'd pursued her. And dangerously intrigued.

Get this over with now.

He'd gone visible again as she walked into the sleeping area. Hands on her hips, she said, "You do that often?"

He shrugged, face impassive. "A gift from the Lady. At certain levels of the Brotherhood, new abilities are earned."

"And I'm sure you're at a stratospheric level nowadays. I hope the goodies were worth it. How did you get in anyway?"

"The locks and other security measures in a place like this offer no challenge. And stealth is a basic skill for the D'nvannae."

"I'm aware." Leaning against the door, she studied him. Part of her wished she'd taken a feelgood. Being alone with him was sending shivers through her and it was hard to concentrate. Hard to breathe. Twilka reached for the anger over how he'd treated her and the emotion drove the tremors from her nerves. *Have to get control of this meeting.* "Hand me my robe, would you?" Taking it from his hand, she slid the soft garment onto her body and strolled to the plush armchair.

Sinking onto the cushions gracefully, crossing her legs, she said, "Your Lady isn't going to visit me too, is she?"

"I pray not. This night is complicated enough." He stepped closer. "You cut your foot on the glass. You're bleeding."

With a wave of nausea, she glanced down. He was right—blood was dripping slowly from her right heel. She hadn't even felt the cut.

"Stay there. I'll get a towel and a packet of skinseal. The hotel does supply a first aid kit, doesn't it?"

"They charge enough, they'd better."

He returned a moment later, kneeling at her feet, holding her foot in one large, warm hand. "Flick the light on." He cleaned the area with a warm washcloth, his touch matter of fact, but the skin to skin contact sent tingles up her leg into more intimate parts of her body. Twilka shifted her hips on the chair's hard cushion and bit her lip. Eyebrow raised, he glanced at her.

"Am I hurting you?"

"No." She shook her head, annoyed with herself for reacting so strongly to him after all this time, and the way he'd abandoned her. "Hurry up, would you?"

"No embedded splinters," he said, drying her foot and then spraying cool skinseal over the wound. He rubbed the area, massaging her toes with one hand while his other hand curled on her calf.

"Enough. I'm fine." Twilka jerked her foot out of his grasp and curled herself protectively in the chair, putting a loose cushion over her stomach. "You wanted to talk, so let's talk."

Khevan studied her silently for a moment before gathering the bloody towel and first aid supplies and taking them to the bathroom. When he emerged, drying his hands, he sat on the edge of the bed.

Waving her hand at him in a sweeping motion, she said, "Not a chance in the seven hells."

"What?" Eyes narrowed, he stared at her.

"Get off my bed. No way are you getting laid here tonight, Brother of the Flames. I'm sure there are more than enough D'nvannae acolytes and groupies at the temple. Go back there. I'm not interested."

"There was a time you were very interested." He rose and moved to the desk chair, spinning it to face her, and sat.

She closed her eyes. Teeth clenched, she said, "Been there, done that, had the experience." Reopening her eyes, she forced her voice into the old lilt. "Don't you know we 'Lites get bored easily? Never repeat a thrill?"

He frowned as if she'd struck him, but then shook his head. "I'm not here to talk about our shared past."

"Anything we shared was so short, the experience isn't worth discussing." But, as she spoke, she realized his hair was now braided. He was under contract. *So why was he here in her room?* A D'nvannae under contract was single minded, wouldn't deviate from the assignment merely to come talk to her.

As if reading her mind, he touched his braid. "I've been hired for a kill."

"Why come and tell me about it?"

"Because you're the target." He kept his gaze on her face, his own calm.

The statement's impact hit her like a burst from a blaster and she fell against the back of her chair, hand at her throat. "Don't try to be funny."

"I'm not joking. The order was delivered to me earlier this evening."

The room closed in around her and she felt lightheaded. Next thing she knew, he had his arms around her, bracing her shoulders. "Breathe," he said. "You're in no danger from me."

"But if you have a kill order…" Her mind was racing, trying to think of a way to escape, despite the utter futility of making an attempt. Khevan could kill her in the blink of an eye. She was a butterfly facing a cobra. Hyperventilating, she was afraid of losing consciousness.

"Now you're breathing too hard. Slow your respiration, calm yourself. Breathe in, hold, breathe out." Holding her firmly, he forced her to meet his stare. "I will never harm you. Surely you know that? How could you imagine anything else?"

"You already tore my heart out," she said, pulling away from him. "Why not kill me?"

Lips in a thin line, he released her with a tiny push and rose, pacing the room as if he was a caged lion. "Who would want you dead?"

"Don't you know who put out the contract?" She ran her hands through her hair, holding her head for a moment, trying to get her mind to stop racing. "Why does it matter? Once the kill order is issued, no one escapes the D'nvannae. It's your Brotherhood's guarantee."

"Our reputation." He smiled, although his face was set in tired lines. "I don't know who set this in motion. Unless the contract is made with a Brother personally, he's never aware who's on the other side. It's none of our business, only the Lady's. Think—what enemies do you have? Family? Business? Romantic rival? Could someone be trying to get revenge on your father for any reason?"

"My dad has thirty-seven kids by an assortment of wives and mistresses. Generational billionaires can afford a giant family. It's a status symbol. I'm not his favorite, not by a long shot. My oldest sister, the one who's being groomed to take over the family business, is at the top of his list, or maybe my twin brothers who run his key subsidiaries in mining and shipping. I'm not even the adored baby of the family." She made a face. "I accepted my spot in the family pecking order long ago and made peace wth how things stand. I'd be the last person a business rival of his would attempt to kill as a means of influencing Arman Zabour. He'd give me a pretty funeral arranged by his personal assistant, attend it as a holo, make a heartfelt speech, and be working interstellar deals five minutes later." Shrugging, she said, "My family is what it is, no use pretending."

"So all the Socialite flamboyance you indulged in at the time we met was acting out? An attempt to get his attention perhaps?"

"We're not analyzing my motivations, not here, not now, not in the middle of the damn night," she said. Rising from the chair, she belted the robe. "Want a drink? I sure need one. And maybe a handful of feelgoods."

He was at her side in an instant, gripping one arm so hard she knew she'd be bruised. "Illicit feelgoods? Is the Combine after you? Did you fall afoul of them?"

"Organized crime?" She laughed in his face. "Hey, people *give* the Socialites their best designer drugs. We make great walking advertisements. I only dabbled in the light stuff—I don't like to lose complete control—and I wasn't a dealer. Personal use only. Gave it all up years ago. After the wreck." Walking to the bar, she wasn't surprised he followed. She poured herself a Taychelle ice vodka on the rocks and filled another glass with Suavarian brandy for him. Pivoting, she offered him the brandy. "This was your drink of choice, I believe."

He took it, draining the glass in one long series of swallows and setting it on the bar with a thump. "Try to take the discussion seriously. This isn't a game."

"I'm not treating it like one. But I need a buzz to offset the terror of having a D'nvannae kill contract on my head." She strolled into the bedroom again. "Romantic rival? Sorry, no joy there. I haven't been involved with anyone seriously since…"

"What about the man on the ship the other night?" His question was fierce.

Twilka laughed. "Jord? Oh, please." Head tilted, hand on her hip, she studied him for a moment, "I was trying to make you jealous, which apparently I did. Nice to know I still hold a little power. Jord and I go way back as friends and now he works for me. Yeah, we slept together a few times before he joined my company, but we found out what we have is a friendship, maybe with occasional benefits, but nothing more."

"How about your business rivals?"

"You have no idea what I do, do you?" she challenged him.

"I see your face everywhere I travel in the Sectors," he said. "Perfume, clothing, jewelry…"

"All thanks to you." Sipping the vodka, she walked to the balcony, avoiding the broken glass on the carpet, and stared at the glowing red temple in the distance. "Or the Red Lady, I guess."

"What do you mean?"

"You left me alone in that damn temple of the White Lady. I had no clothes except the ones on my back and a few shapeless sacks the monks donated. Even belted, they were hopeless." She outlined her figure with one hand. "I'm proud of this body, but it doesn't display well in sacks. I had nothing to do, nowhere to go. Kind of a quiet planet. So one morning while I still had hope I'd see you again, I strolled to the marketplace and bought several lengths of cloth from the local weavers. Paid one of the maids at the monastery to stitch up a few simple dresses from my drawings. Added locally tooled, tasteful leather accessories." She smiled despite the ache in her heart. "I wanted to look decent for you. I can't believe how lost and clueless I was."

He made a move as if he was going to come to her and she neatly stepped around him, heading for the bar and a refill. Over her shoulder, she said, "Once the monks politely booted me out, after it became obvious you'd returned to the Red Lady's embrace, I asked my father to lend me a ship. I flew home and all the press in the Sectors was waiting for me, or so it seemed. Party girl who survived the *Nebula Dream*—what a story, you know? People were clamoring to get their hands on a copy of the dress I wore to the press conference because it was so unique, the prints so dynamic." She tapped her forehead with the rim of the glass. "I'm not dumb, despite what you might think. I recognized an opportunity. I got in touch with Mara, used her contacts in intergalactic trade to buy the entire fabric stock in the town…" She stopped. It had been hard work; she made a lot of mistakes her first year, but she'd had the priceless asset of celebrity as a prominent Socialite already. Add in the fact of being a *Nebula Dream* survivor willing to capitalize on the experience, and the galaxy became the limit. Twilka Enterprises was on its way. "I might not be my father's favorite kid, but I know how to run a business, how to leverage my fame. And he made me a generous loan on good terms. I've even been in a trideo or two, playing myself."

"A role you've perfected." From his tone, it wasn't meant as a compliment. Then he softened it. "I never for a moment considered you unintelligent."

Twilka took a deep breath. "To answer your original question, the fashion business may be cutthroat, but not in the literal sense. The other top designers may envy my success and wish they had my sources, but they're hardly trying to kill me. We each occupy our own niche. So where does my assessment of rivals leave us?"

"In a dire quandary. I would never dishonor the circumstances of our shared past, of all we endured on the *Dream* together, by killing you. Yet, it amused the Red Lady to assign me the contract."

Struck by a terrifying new concern, Twilka asked, "Will she send someone else if I'm not dead in the morning?"

He shook his head. "No. Only one Brother is assigned a task such as this and no one here has the authority to question how I approach the mission. There's no time limit in this case. There are a few Brothers on Temple Home with enough rank to give me orders, and the Red Lady, of course, but I answer to no one else. Certainly no one here on this world."

"So what do we do? I guess we could fake my death, but I might as well *be* dead, if I have to be in hiding the rest of my life. I won't live on the run, in fear." She shook her head. "The one thing the whole *Nebula Dream* experience taught me is how suddenly life can change, can end in the blink of an eye. I live every moment to the fullest and I refuse to give in to fear."

"Except of heights." He flashed her a smile as he referenced a shared memory. "A select few know whether the contract on you was to kill or to guard. The Chief Brother here knows I received an order, but not the nature or who was named, fortunately. His ignorance will buy us time, as long as the Lady doesn't choose to amuse herself further by checking my progress. I pray weightier matters distract her."

"Time to do what exactly?"

"I have allies in the hierarchy at Temple Home. I'll call upon those I trust most to do surreptitious digging, find out who issued this contract to the Brotherhood. Once we know the name, we can figure out what lies at the root of the requested hit, and bargain. Offer the person a high value distraction, an objective or action he or she wants more."

"Or I can take out a hit on them," she said.

He rubbed his chin and eyed her speculatively. "It wouldn't be unheard of, but expensive."

"I was joking." Mouth open, she stared at him.

"I'm not."

She swallowed. "Okay, well let's hope this is a mistake, and once you know who hates me enough to kill me, we can buy them off, distract them with something they think is sparkly. Are you going to get in touch with me when you know the name?"

"I'm not leaving your side until this is resolved. You have a D'nvannae body-guard." He gave her a formal bow. "Although no other D'nvannae will be sent, the mere fact someone wants you dead speaks to the need for your protection."

You protecting me was all I ever wanted. Once. "Tomorrow..." She glanced at the wall chrono, noting the local time. "Today I mean, I have a series of meetings with buyers, suppliers, influential customers—I may be the best advertisement for my own lines, but there are men and women it's essential to have wearing my clothes—crowned by my fashion show in the evening and a blowout party to celebrate." She made a face. "All business, unfortunately. Nothing like the parties I used to attend. This week is the biggest event in the Sectors' high fashion industry. You'll be bored out of your mind." She winced as a thought struck her. "There'll be masses of press in the evening venue who will be very interested in why I suddenly have a D'nvannae bodyguard. And if—when—the reporters connect the dots to realize you're the Brother from the *Nebula Dream*..." She shook her head. "We managed to hide the fact we were together then, brief though the attachment was." She hoped he couldn't detect the pain triggered by the memory. "But this will be big news."

He slashed his hand as if fending off an opponent. "No press. The Lady pays no attention to ephemeral things like fashion," he said with disdain, "But if there was enough publicity involving me, the fact might come to her ears. I have rivals, enemies in the hierarchy." He tapped his fingers on the arm of the chair. "As one rises higher in her favor, opportunities for further advancement become limited; there are fierce power struggles, which she relishes. Only a few men can ever enjoy the ultimate spot as a personal companion to the Lady, involved in running the Brotherhood."

"And that's what you always wanted, isn't it? I guess I should feel honored you'd risk a place at her side to save me for old times' sake." Yawning, she said, "Since you assure me I'm safe, I need to get a few hours of sleep. So what's the plan? Are you going to be front and center on view, or do your invisibility trick, or what?"

"The cloaking cannot be sustained for more than a few moments. I'll stay in the background as much as possible. And I gave no interviews, was only recorded by the press in passing after the wreck, when my tariqna had been removed by the Lady. We should be fine."

"True. You do look different with the tattoo." She ran her fingers through her hair like a comb. "Maybe the press will think it's a publicity stunt. I'm known for crazy stuff—the media says everyone speculates what I'll do for attention next." Pointing her finger at him, she made her voice icy. "We're not sharing the bed by the way—you can have the couch in the sitting room. I've got a breakfast strategy session with my assistant and Jord first thing, though, so we'll be up early."

"You'll explain nothing to them."

"You don't get to give me orders. I appreciate your refusal to kill me, but that doesn't mean you get to tell me what to do."

He came close, lifting one hand to touch her hair. "You let your hair grow."

Twilka laughed. "I've changed color and style fifty times at least in the last five years. I thought you said you've seen my merchandise ads? This is actually close to my real hair color, as best I remember."

He shook his head, letting the curl drop from his fingers. "You appear different. Softer."

"Don't let the hair fool you. I'm still my father's daughter and I can cut a deal like nobody's business."

"Let's hope you can demonstrate the skill on whoever issued the contract." He snagged a pillow and a spare blanket from the bed and left the room before she could think of a suitable retort.

CHAPTER THREE

Contrary to Twilka's expectations, the day began smoothly. Lissa and Jord were shocked to find Khevan installed in Twilka's hotel room, but she offered no explanation or even an introduction, so her employees exchanged puzzled glances and settled down to work. Despite his claim to be her bodyguard, he was in and out of the room Twilka used as a temporary office, apparently working his private communications channels, trying to find out who had ordered her death.

Taking her cue from him, and because she couldn't maintain a state of fight or flight indefinitely, Twilka managed to conduct her business efficiently. It was a relief to concentrate on fabrics and orders and minor problems with the big show scheduled for the evening.

Then it was time to get dressed for the presentation. Khevan waited in the living area.

Twilka took a deep breath and stepped out. His eyes widened and she heard him inhale sharply, but he said nothing. "Well?" She pirouetted on her sky high heels, allowing the diaphanous dress to swirl around her. "The skirt fabric is from Temple Home, the bodice is constructed from Kildar Six iridescent spider webs. I'm not allowing anyone else to buy this model—it's a Twilka Original and exclusive. To me." She laughed.

"Dress and woman are exceptional," he said with gallantry, coming to take her elbow. "Tell me again what we're doing this evening?"

"You never used to make pretty remarks like that. Picked up a new skill, have you?" She twisted her arm slightly to dislodge his hand. As he backed off, she went to the mirror to dust a final finishing coat of cosmetic over her lips. "It's a show, of my gowns and those by nine other top designers," she said over her shoulder. "A glittering affair. The proceeds go to a variety of charities. Ostensibly the show is for people to place orders, but of course I've already contracted for all this collection's sales. The business can't wait for the pageantry. I may book a few selected individual orders though." She scooped up her purse and threw her personal AI inside. "We're doing this same show in several Sector hubs, with a rotating cast of designers and it's being beamed Sectorswide as entertainment. We—the fashion council—instituted this a few years ago. Apparently it was a custom on Old Terra at one point." She shrugged. "The old becomes new again if you wait long enough. Then the party afterward is where the fashion community mixes and mingles, gossips and networks. And drinks or does feelgoods. The important thing is to be seen."

"And this is your life now?" he asked, as she exited the suite ahead of him.

"Well at least I don't go around killing people," she said. "I have precious downtime in between designing new collections. Not much, but enough to visit friends, do a little sightseeing, keep my eyes out for new inspiration and fresh ideas. I occupy my time doing a mix of things and rarely party, except in connection with the business."

"Are you often bored?"

Laughing at the idea, she said, "Rarely. Turns out I love the creative process. The business not so much, although there's a certain satisfaction in negotiating a good deal, or getting my product into a new market. A girl has to keep busy. And if I'm not going to party and do feelgoods all the time, might as well be a fashion magnate. I do a bare minimum of the party and celebrity circuit to keep my Socialite cred. It's a key part of my brand."

They descended the stairs in silence. Twilka refused to do the hotel gravlift—any gravlift—so she did a lot of stair climbing, often in precarious heels, like tonight. Her calves and thighs were killer as a result.

The media was waiting as she exited the lobby to get into her groundcar. Khevan shifted into full bodyguard mode, establishing a path for her to walk unmolested. People shied away from him instinctively—no one wanted to risk annoying a D'nvannae. She heard a few shouted questions about the new security measures, but ignored them with practiced ease and a big smile, accented by waves to a few of the reporters she knew as she got into the waiting vehicle. Lissa and Jord were already inside and her assistant handed her a glass of champagne as soon as she sat down. Khevan filled the entire bench seat across from her. He really was larger than life, all hard muscle and grim determination. Five years had dimmed her memories a bit.

Lissa stared at him, open mouthed. Jord said, "Sorry, we didn't pour a glass for you…"

"He's working; didn't you see the braid? Ignore him," Twilka said. She and her staff clinked glasses. "Here's to a good show. You've checked the venue?"

As Lissa recited a summary of the pros and cons of the place where the exclusive fashion show was to be held, Twilka sat and sipped her drink. She would have preferred to check it out herself earlier, as she usually did, but Khevan was adamant she keep her appearances outside the hotel suite to a minimum, since he would have to accompany her, and the goal was to keep his presence low key. She realized Lissa had asked her a question, and she and Jord were staring at her expectantly.

"Sorry, thinking about a new design. What did you say?"

"I know you like to indulge your creative urge at all times of the day and night, boss lady, but you need to focus on the business tonight." Jord plucked the champagne from her hand. "She *said* Fiona Montecouer is attending tonight's gala and has asked for a gown to wear from the collection. A private fitting, before the show. She and her people will be meeting us there in half an hour, standard time."

Twilka stared at him. *What's with this attitude?* Was proximity to Khevan raising Jord's jealous hackles? She so didn't have time for this tonight. She stifled an urge to giggle at the mental picture of Jord squaring off with Khevan. Sure he'd been an all Sectors tisba striker and had kept his six pack through assiduous training ever since retiring with an injury, but he'd be no match for a D'nvannae Brother. No one would be. "I don't have time to pamper a demanding celebrity before the show."

Lissa shook her head. "We've been trying to get her into your clothes for three seasons now. You have to accommodate her."

I don't have to do anything. The rebellious urge rose in her like hot lava. A headache began to throb and she rubbed her left temple.

"Besides, she just had that incredible hit trideo; she's a sure thing for the Best Actress nomination and we need her to be in a Twilka Original." Lissa made her case.

Khevan was watching her, face impassive. Twilka wondered what he thought of her business. Straightening, she said, "Of course you're right, although everyone knows Liora will win for the biopic of the Angel of Fantalar."

"Liora doesn't have the right image for your brand and Fiona does," Lissa said. "She appeals to the edgy Socialite wannabees, especially since she never hides the fact she came up from some awful colony somewhere. People can't be *you*, but they can sure relate to being her. Her patronage is a fusion that can boost us."

Pondering whether Lissa was planning to do a sneaky side deal, hire a designer, and attempt to steal a good chunk of Twilka's clientele, she gave in. *Good luck because no other celebrity designer has my connection to the wreck of the* Nebula Dream *and people are still fascinated by that night to remember. And by me because I survived. Fiona may be a poor kid who hit the big time, but she's easily replaced. No one else will ever be me, lucky for them.* "All right, if it'll make you happy, Fiona can have half an hour."

There was no horde of press to navigate at the venue because the groundcar deposited them at a side entrance. Twilka swept inside and was immediately plunged into the chaos of preparing for a major show. Two of the models were having a catfight over who should wear the show opener, which wasn't their decision in any event. She settled the squabble in a heartbeat, by switching the dress in question to a third girl, and stepped aside to confer with the event's Master of Ceremonies. The entire contingent of models was staring at Khevan and trying to get his attention, some more subtly than others, but he was focused on Twilka. She could tell, although he was acting like a bodyguard, assessing the environment and all the people in it with a cold eye, watching for threats. His presence would be comforting, if it didn't arouse all kinds of other emotions and memories she could definitely do without.

The trideo star swept in with her entourage and her bodyguards, who seemed like untested boys next to Khevan. Twilka escorted the group to a private space at the edge of the fashion maelstrom, and dresses were brought to be tried on. In under half an hour the celebrity was satisfied, walking out in a gown Twilka decreed suited her perfectly and would land Fiona in all the "best of" trideo streams, garnering priceless publicity for the actress and for Twilka. She lingered behind for a moment, sinking into a handy chair.

"Is it always this manic?" Khevan asked, moving behind her to rub her shoulders.

Rolling her head from side to side in sheer relief as the muscle tension eased, she said, "Your hands work magic. Is massage normally part of the D'nvannae bodyguard service?"

"No. But I can see you getting tense and from what you've said, there are hours of this event left to get through." He lifted his hands away from her body as Lissa burst through the door with a quick knock.

Open mouthed, she stared from one to the other. "Oh, sorry." Obviously recalling her errand, she said hesitantly, "I hate to interrupt, but the model tore the green sheath, put her foot right through the hem, and the girl for the purple-and-gold ball gown hasn't arrived yet..."

"You may have to wear the dress and walk yourself," Twilka said, rising. "It wouldn't be the first time. Have we briefed the models on how I want them to strut this year?" Lissa nodded. "Good. Let's go see how bad the damage is. Maybe we can stitch on trim to hide the tear in the green."

"The seamstresses are all busy adjusting hems and taking in seams. There's not going to be enough time…"

"I haven't forgotten how to use a needle." Twilka made a little sewing motion as she walked.

"And the girl who's supposed to wear the finale piece hasn't arrived yet." Lissa had the tone of a person with a long list of problems to report. "I heard she got hired to walk in another show and might not be here for us at all."

"Let me see who's in the first third of the program that can do a quick change and we'll pick a new girl for the finale." Twilka brushed past a pair of stylists with arms full of accessories. "What else? I know you're not done dumping catastrophes on me."

Her assistant stopped dead. "How do you *do* that? Are you sure you don't have psychic powers?"

Laughing in spite of her tension, Twilka grabbed Lissa by the elbow and dragged her out of the way of a stage tech burdened down with complicated equipment. "Just a lot of experience with these productions. I've seen it all at least ten times over the years. Nothing surprises me."

"This might." Lissa took a deep breath. "So the Evanderly people staged a living vignette? And the models had to be part of the scenery?"

Nodding, Twilka walked faster, anxious to deal with the green dress and then the rest of the problems. "A bit over the top, but the collection was too simple. He needed something to distract the critics. How does that affect me?"

"Three of our girls have a purple rash from the leaves and insects they had to wear."

Hands on her hips, Twilka blinked. "Okay, that is new. Can we cover them with glittering stardust powder?"

"Depending which dresses they're supposed to wear." Biting her lip, Lissa considered.

Twilka gave her assistant a tiny shove. "Go figure it out with the head makeup artist. He'll love the challenge, even as he cusses you out. And then get Jord away from the catering tables and tell him to supervise the dressers like he's supposed to be doing. I'm off to take care of the green dress."

The pace of problems and calls for her personal attention were nonstop. At five minutes to curtain, Lissa reported the venue was full, people clamoring for seats, standing room only. "And we're already booking orders for the dress you let Fiona have!"

The music started pumping. Twilka moved to the edge of the stage, took a deep breath, and walked out to welcome the audience to her show. She couldn't really see them for all the lights and she had a moment of sheer panic, terrified whoever had taken out the contract on her life might be here, tired of waiting for the D'nvannae to take action. She heard herself uttering her pretty speech of thanks, using the old lilting Socialite voice and plenty of the current slang, because that was still the bedrock of her image—'Lite girl gone legit—applause crescendoed and she was safely backstage again as the first model sashayed onto the runway, perfect face set in a contemptuous mask, as if to say other people could buy the dress, but no one could wear it as well as she did.

Khevan was behind her. She could feel his massive presence like the gravity of a major planet and the thought was reassuring. Models sauntered by in an endless stream, apparently untouched by the backstage chaos. Twilka made a few last second adjustments, but for the most part merely watched, taking mental notes about accessories. The constant applause was reassuring. Lissa came to stand at her shoulder, edging around Khevan in an unintentionally comical maneuver.

"Another hit," she whispered into Twilka's ear.

Nodding, Twilka waited for the last gown, a confection of white lace with a black and purple accent to give it the necessary fashion edge, to make its second appearance as the show ended, and stepped out at the right interval behind the girl, waving to the crowd and smiling to acknowledge their kudos. A bow at the end of the runway and she and the model pranced backstage, hand in hand, as if they were best friends since childhood. A wave and a blown kiss from the curtain's edge and she was done. People crowded her, hugging her and saying nice things about the show, the gathering giddy on an adrenaline high. Customers, critics, rivals, and friends flooded the area, coming to offer their congratulations. Twilka floated through the gathering as she'd done many times before.

Suddenly, Khevan had her by the arm, leading her away from a circle of perplexed guests and into the private space at the rear of their portion of the venue. He shut the door, leaning on it as if to block a horde of Mawreg from gaining entry. "We have to leave *now*."

"What are you talking about? We can go back to the hotel for a few hours in between the show and tonight's gala, but I have at least another hour of accepting congratulations, air kissing, and sipping champagne before we're done here." She sank into the chair, rubbing her ankle. "I don't mind taking a moment to rest, but I can't spare too much time."

He advanced to the chair, caging her in the seat with his powerful arms. "I found out who issued the contract for your death. It was the Red Lady herself. And she's sent a compliance squad to ensure I complete the assignment."

"Why?" Shocked, she could barely form the words. "After all these years, why target me now? What the seven hells have I done to her?"

He shook his head. "It's not you; it's me. She's decided to test me in consideration for promotion to the next level; it's what she does…"

Twilka saw red. She shoved him violently away, which even in the moment she knew was only possible because he was off balance and unwilling to exert his strength against her. "I'm the one she wants dead." She sprang from the chair and paced. "Why would killing me prove anything to her? You walked away from me of your own accord without a backward glance five years ago. I mean nothing to you."

"That's not true," he said.

She stopped in mid-step and stared. "Which part? Because from my viewpoint, it's all true."

He averted his gaze rather than meet her angry eyes, an evasive act so astounding and out of character that she caught her breath. *What is he hiding?*

Clearing his throat, he said, "We don't have time to discuss this now. If there's a compliance squad assigned to me, they may already be here on the planet. The enforcers may have arrived before I did. In fact, I'd bet on it, remembering the way the Chief Monk was acting when he handed me the order. He possessed knowledge disadvantageous to me. We have to go to ground and hide, right now. Then figure out how to extricate ourselves." Fists clenched, he looked ready for combat.

"So I have to die to prove you're worthy of—of what? Fucking her?"

"Twilka, please, I'll be happy to answer any question, but not now." He held out one hand. "Can you trust me as you once did?"

She stared at him as if he was a snake and brushed his hand aside with an angry slap. "Why don't I go the Sector authorities and get protection, get transported off planet? Or drive to the White Lady's temple here and ask for sanctuary? While you and the fire bitch play your games and work this out."

He shook his head. "The Sectors won't get involved in a legitimate contract issue involving the Red Lady. There's a treaty, remember? As to your other idea, the Lady in White doesn't maintain a personal presence here, despite the temple. There's no one on this planet of sufficient standing in her hierarchy to agree to assist you. I doubt the head monk there would even let you into his facility—he won't want to accept the risk."

"She was ready to help both of us five years ago and you threw it all away."

Twilka watched him visibly control his anger at her continued barbs. For her part, she was barely restraining herself from hurling things at him. The old pain of rejection was like poison in her heart, compounded by her current jeopardy and the knowledge he was hiding something.

"The compliance squad will kill you and then execute me if we let ourselves be caught," he said. "My informant at Temple Home was able to tell me that much before he was cut off in mid transmission. I fear he's dead. I told you I have rivals, and I think this kill scenario with you at the center was contrived to force my hand. Someone's attempting a power grab and you're the convenient pawn." He took a deep breath. "We can argue later if you desire. Right now we have to go. The entire population of the Sectors knows where you are at this moment, thanks to the media." He frowned, eyeing her. "But not in that dress and those shoes."

She threw her hair off her shoulders with a sweeping gesture and snorted contemptuously. "I'll be even more noticeable naked. What do you suggest? Do we risk a stop at the hotel?"

"No. We'll certainly be taken if we go there." He gazed around the tiny office, as if expecting a solution to appear from thin air.

Twilka jumped, hand at her throat, as the door panel vibrated under a vigorous pounding. "Boss lady? We need you out here, now," Jord said through the closed panel. "Are you okay?"

Watching Khevan, she raised her voice to answer, "Just the damn recurring headache. Give me a minute for the headclear to work and I'll join you. Go find Fiona, would you? And set up a photo op?"

"Will do." She heard the sound of his footsteps retreating down the short hall.

"Go out there and grab me some clothes and a pair of shoes from the models' changing stations," she said to Khevan. "The girls come in wearing rags—it's like a law of nature, the more elevated the fashions to be shown, the more downmarket the models act." She made a shooing motion and then reached to unfasten her dress. "Hurry up. I'll be right here."

He slipped out the door and returned a moment or two later, bearing a clingy top, a big overshirt, and a pair of tight leggings. He had a pair of sensible, scuffed shoes under his arm. Twilka grabbed the items and got dressed as fast as she could. She wasn't surprised to find he'd gotten things close enough to her size to fit. Thorough was the D'nvannae style. Pulling a scarf from an overflowing box of accessories by the door, she fastened her hair into a casual ponytail. Grabbing her elegant, bejeweled purse, she frowned. Dumping the contents on the desk in a messy pile, she took her personal AI and a few other necessities, stuffing them into the pockets of the overshirt.

"Leave the AI," he said. "You can be traced."

"Not with this model. My father's IT squad directs their best efforts into maintaining security of the family's hardware. I need to be able to communicate. Let's go."

He opened the door a crack. "Coast is clear." Slipping out, he checked to be sure she was behind him. "The least observed exit is at the rear, a service dock. I've disabled the surveillance cameras."

"Show me the way."

Twilka on his heels, Khevan skulked through the venue's machinery rooms, jogged through hallways, dodged in and out of storerooms full of props, eventually emerging on a grimy dock. One massive cargo hauler sat idling off to the side, no sign of the driver.

"Are we going to steal the truck?" She thought that might be exciting, but Khevan jumped from the loading platform and assisted her to the ground, after which he kept hold of her hand and ran past the vehicle.

"This isn't an adventure trideo," he said, his voice stern. "We can lose ourselves in the city much more efficiently on foot."

He assisted her in sneaking through a gap in the fence and heading along the deserted road into the depths of the city.

"Do we have a plan?" she asked. "Aren't you kind of conspicuous, tattoo and all?"

"There are D'nvannae coming and going in this city, and most civilians can't read the tattoos, so a person in the street wouldn't distinguish me from any other brother. The immediate plan is to travel deep into the transient area by the spaceport, hole up in a cheap anonymous room, and figure out what to do next."

CHAPTER FOUR

Two hours later, after weaving and winding through several of the more disreputable areas of the city, Twilka stood next to the sagging bed in the middle of a tiny room, her arms crossed defiantly over her chest. "I'm afraid to touch anything—this place is probably brimming with germs and disgusting substances. And the creepy proprietor could be a mass murderer, from the expression he was wearing." She shivered. "I've never seen such dead eyes on a person who was still breathing. He's addicted to something." Everywhere she looked in the room there were unpleasant reminders of how awful this place was—stains on the industrial carpet, holes in the wall, even a multi-legged insect crawling up one side of the door. "How long are we staying here?"

Khevan ignored her question as he unpacked the bag of food he'd purchased from a street vendor. He offered her a wrapped chamile roaster leg, dripping with sauce. "Hungry? We can think better on a full stomach."

"I'll think better if I'm buzzed. I need something to reduce my stress level. Where's the beer you bought?" She took the avian drumstick and sat on the only chair, which creaked alarmingly as she allowed the seat to take her weight. He handed her an open container and Twilka took a long drink.

Munching on his food, Khevan put some credits in the tiny vid screen embedded in the wall, which activated in fits and starts. He set the selection to local news. There was nothing about Twilka during the brief program.

"Good. Lissa and Jord are probably frantic right now, but trying to keep this from becoming a full-blown disaster. People will talk when I'm not at the party tonight, but hopefully there'll be a new juicy scandal or upset to distract the media. The reporters who follow celebrities have the attention span of small furry mammals. Easily drawn to a new novelty." Twilka deposited the remnants of her dinner in the dispose-all and drained the beer. "My staff won't report my being missing to the authorities until tomorrow, if at all." She shrugged. "The benefit of being known as a flighty 'Lite, who takes it into her head to do wild pranks. Never mind I haven't done anything crazy in years. A well-crafted reputation like I've got lives forever. You'd think I'd done it all on purpose in my younger years so I could coast in my old age. I only wish I'd been that smart." Hands on her hips, she stared at Khevan. "Despite my pleasant demeanor, I'm about out of patience, I warn you. Ready to talk now?"

"I'm sorry I got you into this," he said.

"A little late for apologies." She glared at the bed with distaste. "I'm supposed to be at a gala party in a glamorous dress designed by me, working the crowd, drinking expensive feelgoods, and drumming up new business by the shipload. Maybe flirting with cute trideo stars or investors and being photographed. Instead I'm in this dump, in stolen clothes I wouldn't wear for a night crawling through dive bars, and I'm with you. Oh, and with a contract out on my head." She squared her shoulders. "So, who are we going to get to help us? I can call my father, but I don't think he has influence with the Red Lady. How many credits would it take to get her to back off?"

"At best, he could hire civilian bodyguards for you, maybe get you off the planet for now if he moved fast enough, but she'd find you eventually. Since this is personal with her, your father could hand over the entire Sectors' government treasury and she wouldn't call off the hunt. I think there's only one person I can ask for help for both of us, and yet I'm not sure what he can do."

Dusting the surface of the bed cover off with a frown, examining her hand for a moment, Twilka sat on the end of the bed. "Nick Jameson."

"Yes. After the *Nebula Dream*, he swore to come to my aid if ever I needed him, and I made a matching oath. Although how he can help..."

"You may be surprised. After the first year, once he left the military, he and Mara established a couple of businesses. She runs a shipping operation and he has a high level, hush hush security firm. Lot of ex Special Forces types working for him and some unusual...consultants. I heard he might even have an in with the Mellureans. Aren't they the only ones who can stand up to your Red Lady besides her sister? Hey, what about appealing to them ourselves? She didn't much like me, but you and Lady Damais sure bonded..." She looked at his face and stopped. "What? What did I say?"

"How do you know about what Nick and Mara are doing?"

"*You* may have cut off communication with all of us, but I stayed in touch with them. I've spent time at their home, in fact. The Jamesons are at peace with the world. Although they do keep busy." She dug her personal AI out of the pocket in her oversize shirt. "Do you need their contact data?"

"Were you always this practical, underneath the 'Lite façade?"

"I don't know," she said honestly. "What with my father's fortune and my friends, life was a continuous, moving party and I drifted with it. No one expected me to do anything else. After the wreck, after you abandoned me, I couldn't re-enter the old world I used to play in. I didn't fit in. I can pretend for a while, long enough to do my commercials and sell my bits and pieces. I can make a speech at the start of a fashion show. Maybe someday I'll tell you more about that, if we survive and if I'm still talking to you. Are we going to call Nick or not?"

"Go ahead."

"We'll have to send a message, no vids at this distance, not even with the network my father owns. What do you want me to say?"

"Calling in the favor, situation red tinged and deadly. He'll get the gist. You can add we need help to get off the planet and hide while we try to solve this."

"Cryptic but pithy. I like it." She sent the message. "We'll probably hear back in a few hours, based on past experiences, and if he's available, not off on a mission. No one who works for him could handle this, so I tagged it for his eyes only. Or Mara's."

"We'll have to hope we hear soon. Evading the Brotherhood is going to get more and more challenging as the hours pass." He assessed her from head to toe, but there was no emotion showing on his face. "You must be tired. Why don't you get some sleep?"

She eyed the bed with distaste. "I'm not getting under those covers."

"Lay on top of them. Here, you can use my jacket as a blanket." He handed over his black leather jacket, still warm from his body.

She kicked off her borrowed shoes and curled up in the sagging center of the cheap mattress. Unable to stop herself, she took a deep breath, inhaling his scent, which clung to the lining of the jacket, a delicious, exotic blend reminiscent of pine trees and spices, with a sharp citrus note, underscored by the clean scent of his own skin. She'd never been able to resist the enticement of his scent, the smooth feel of his skin, his hard muscles pressed against her soft core… Annoyed with herself and the way her body was reacting, Twilka pushed the jacket aside. She didn't need complications, or the heartbreak, when he walked away again once their problem was resolved. Yawning, she rolled onto her other side and forced her churning anxieties into the pattern of her best meditation, hoping sleep would come soon.

She was trapped in the corridor, spine pressed to the bulkhead, surrounded by a pack of faceless men, laughing, leering, grabbing at her. The other woman, the one they'd attacked first, before Twilka stumbled across the gathering in her desperate search for a lifeboat, lay unmoving on the deck…As the ringleader lunged forward and grabbed her, Twilka screamed curses, striking out in self-defense.

"Ssh, you're safe with me." Khevan held her tight, easily blocking her instinctive blows, crooning calming words.

Disoriented, she collapsed against his shoulder and let herself be comforted. The warmth of his body against hers was soothing and she curled one leg over his, pulling him closer.

"I had a hard time waking you and you're still shaking. Do you have the old nightmare often?" He rubbed her lower back, slowly.

"Not anymore. Maybe a few times a month. Always the same—the damn corridor on the *Nebula Dream*, the one by the casino, you know? And I know no one's going to help me…"

"But we did." His voice rumbled against her ear.

"Dreams aren't logical," she said, allowing herself one more moment in his arms. "I don't think I'm trying to relive the actual incident. The push from my subconscious is constant, probably symbolic of deeper issues." She pulled away from him and scrambled off the bed, feeling self-conscious and undignified.

"What kind of issues?"

"Facing life without you. Not being able to trust you, if you must know." She escaped into the tiny bathroom and shut the door. Leaning on the sink, she wiped away angry tears. *I used to hope he'd come back into my life, then I moved on because the pain of it was so overwhelming. Why do I have to deal with him now?* Staring into the spotted mirror for a moment, she admitted to herself she was lying about getting over Khevan. *But I did move on.*

He knocked on the door. "Are you all right?"

"I don't suffer nightmares when I'm awake," she said before washing her face and reluctantly using the skimpy towel. "What time is it anyway? I can't go to sleep after the dream. My nerves are fried, so if you want the bed now, be my guest. D'nvannae probably need rest too, whether you'd ever admit it or not."

When she re-emerged, he was stretched out on the bed, hands at his sides, eyes closed. With determination, she sat at the desk, facing away from him, and worked on new designs for next year's line, creating tiny 3D sketches with her AI that floated in the air around her as she completed each one, until finally she was so exhausted she lowered her head to the hard surface and slept.

In the morning he left the room without comment, returning a few moments later with the breakfast he'd obtained from nearby street vendors. "We're going to have to move today," he said as he parceled out the food onto the desk, which was the only surface in the room other than the bed.

Twilka paused as she reached for a cup of steaming hot liquid she desperately hoped was caffeinated. "Why? Did you see something suspicious on the street?"

"No, but the desk clerk is entirely too interested in me. It might be the novelty of seeing a D'nvannae in this low level place, or it might be more. Wouldn't surprise me if the temple circulated word among the criminal elements to watch for me. The Brotherhood makes use of local informants at times. But we can eat first. You have to keep your strength up if we're going to stay ahead of pursuit."

She opened her mouth to urge they leave now, but there was a ping from her AI. "Incoming message," she said, checking the device. "It's from Nick. He says hang tight, he can be here the day after tomorrow and will send instructions for a discreet meetup." She felt the tension leaving her body, tight back and neck muscles loosening and relaxing at the mere thought of Nick Jameson's arrival to help them. Her headache receded.

Khevan sipped his synthcaff, brow furrowed in a frown. "Two days is a long time to stay on the run when the Brotherhood is hunting."

"Could have been longer. Nick must have been somewhere relatively close." Twilka shut her AI and slid it into her pocket. "We deserve a piece of good luck." Knowing Nick was on his way to them raised her spirits significantly. No situation ever daunted the former soldier for long, no matter how dire. He always found a way through, over or under any challenge.

After breakfast, she packed her meager belongings and watched as Khevan used a special Brotherhood device to erase all submolecular physical traces of their presence. Then they headed out, descending a few floors on the emergency stairs and then crossing through the building before going the rest of the way to the ground floor. She emerged on the less traveled rear service street and raised her face to the slight breeze to clear the scent of institutional disinfectant from her lungs. The maintenance staff at the hotel obviously thought splashing quantities of the stuff in the rooms and corridors made up for any other lack of housekeeping.

Khevan said, "We'll spend a few hours in the bazaar, get lost in the crowds. I can see if anyone is tailing us." He took her elbow and guided her east, toward the teeming streets where merchandise of all sorts was sold. The crowds were thick today, which was a scheduled day of rest on this planet. Twilka stuck close to his side as the throngs made way for him. She feigned interest in whatever he told her to admire when he needed an opportunity to check their backtrail and found a few things she made mental notes to send her assistant to buy, if she survived this whole adventure. Her sense of unreality about the past two days was strong.

She was going through a pile of fabrics in the midafternoon, enjoying the patterns and the tactile pleasure of the varied fibers against her skin, waiting for him to rejoin her, after which they were going to find another flea bag temporary residence and go to ground for the night. She was hot and sweaty, her legs hurt, and she was tired of being jostled. Closing her eyes for a moment, she yearned wistfully for her luxury suite at the hotel, the giant bathtub with massage jets, the bed just firm enough for her liking. And no insects.

She looked over her shoulder to see if Khevan was on his way to rejoin her yet and her nagging problems fled as she observed him standing fifty feet away, talking to another D'nvannae Brother. Adrenaline banished all traces of tiredness. *Is he betraying me?* The suspicion ran through her like a shock of ice water.

The other man was younger, his tattoo not nearly as well defined, and the men weren't facing in her direction. Twilka slid behind two larger women debating the merits of a hideous furry orange fabric and pressed her back to the wall. Peering out, she couldn't see Khevan's face, but she didn't like the smirk on the other Brother's countenance. Trying to control her breathing, she was frozen for a moment, debating what to do. *Should I get away from Khevan now? Wait for Nick on my own?* This could all be a cruel trick on the part of the Red Lady, with Khevan fully on board to torment her for his goddess's pleasure. A twisted mind game would be the Lady's style.

Arguing with herself, panic lacing the edge of her nerves, she took a second glance at the two Brothers, now standing as if ready to fight each other. Clearly the discussion wasn't going well.

I trust him. Whatever happened five years ago, I believe his promise not to carry out the contract on me. Strategically, she worked her way down the street toward the two men, using the crowd as cover, trying to stay out of the other D'nvannae's line of sight. Moving in and out of vendor stalls, she got within a few feet of the pair, close enough to hear their low, tense conversation. The discussion wasn't in any language she understood, so Twilka hesitated to intervene or announce her presence. Khevan moved to walk away from his compatriot and the other man deployed a curved knife so smoothly the movement seemed like magic.

Khevan shoved the man's blow aside with a sharp defensive parry and the opponents retreated a few feet from each other, faces set in grim lines, clearly about to duel in the street.

There were gasps and a few screams, and many of the more timid in the crowd surged to flee the immediate vicinity, temporarily knocking Twilka aside. Clawing her way to a new vantage point, she saw Khevan had his own knife out now and had clearly drawn blood. His opponent was snarling what sounded like curses or taunts as the men circled each other, ready to exploit any opening. Khevan stayed grimly silent. Another flurry of clashing knives and well-aimed kicks had her scared to death, clenched fist to mouth. She wanted desperately to find a way to help Khevan, but only an idiot got between two deadly men.

"Unusual sport, to see two of them fight," said a man behind her. "Twenty credits on the younger Brother."

"Fight won't last long enough to know who wins," said the bald man next to the first speaker. "Temple forces will be here any minute now, break it up, make them take the quarrel to a private place. Bad for the Red Lady's reputation, her men fighting among themselves."

"Over a woman," the original would-be gambler explained. "Heard them talking before the knives came out."

Twilka sidled away as the men continued to gossip. If reinforcements were coming from the Temple, she had to get Khevan and herself gone. Now. A stack of ripe kochani nuts, each as big as a Terran apple, sat on the table next to her and she grabbed one. Bouncing it in her hand for a moment to judge the weight, she stepped forward, out of the crowd, took aim, and flung the nut with deadly accuracy, striking the younger Brother in the forehead. He recoiled, blinking as if dazed, and glared at the crowd. She threw a second one, aiming for his forehead and hitting his temple instead.

The younger Brother fell and Khevan ran to her, grabbing her away from the gawking cluster of startled citizens. Dragging her by the wrist, he sprinted past the moaning man in the street, taking a sharp left into an alley and cutting through another area of the bazaar. "Quick thinking," he said over his shoulder. "Where did you learn to throw so accurately?"

"One of my half-brothers plays professional ball," she said in between gasping breaths. "I was bored one summer and he was on injured reserve so he taught me. Can we stop for a moment?"

"All right." He skidded to a halt in between two buildings and she bent over, struggling to inhale enough air to renew the run. "He was trying to delay me, keep me there until the Temple forces arrived."

"Yeah, the people I was standing with said the Brothers would be coming soon. Concussing him with a hard object to the head was the only thing I could think of to help you." As she straightened, breathing more easily, she did a double take, reaching out one hand to his abdomen, where red blood was dripping through a tear in his shirt. "Lords of Space, you're injured. How bad is it?"

"He got in a lucky slash," Khevan said, face set in tense lines. "A mere scratch."

"Let me see."

"Not here." He pushed her away. "We've got to put more distance between us and them." He pulled his jacket closed and applied pressure to the wound with his hand. "I'll manage."

"Can we steal a groundcar maybe?" Twilka fell into step beside him as he walked down the alley toward the next street.

He glanced at her. "We don't want the local police involved. If you or I, or both of us, were confined in jail, the Lady would extract us like clams from a shell. Treaties, remember?" He staggered a little. "Civilian authorities would have to yield to her. You'd be dead soon after walking out of the cell."

Concerned as he staggered slightly, she put her arm around his waist. "You're not doing well; we need to hole up and take care of the wound. Now."

He assessed the surrounding area. "We must go deeper into the slum, then obtain an automated rent-by-the-hour room and stay there for the night. No more nosy desk clerks. I have fake ID we can use to secure the room."

Arm in arm as if they were lovers, she and Khevan strolled through the trash-filled streets, rejecting the first few rent-a-room places before Twilka decided enough was enough and booked a chamber with his fake ID. The robo clerk delivered a card key and she led Khevan to the designated unit, breathing a deep sigh of relief as the door closed behind them and they were out of the public eye.

"Let me see your injury," she said, as he sank onto the none too generous bed.

The slash looked dangerous to her, the edges red and puffy. "Do D'nvannae ever coat their blades with poison?" She asked the question over her shoulder as she went into the tiny bathroom to search for something to wash the wound with.

"A treachery against our code of honor. Such an act would only be done at the Lady's express command, and the Brother I met in the street wasn't part of a compliance squad sent by her. I taught his class at the local temple in the afternoon before the kill order arrived, so he recognized me." Khevan removed his shirt as she approached with cloths. "I think he overestimated his own abilities and hoped to earn renown by being the one to turn me in. A smarter move would have been to stay out of sight, call for assistance, and attempt to follow us."

He clenched his jaw and bore her attempts at first aid in silence, merely tugging his shirt over the clumsy bandages she made from strips of her shirt when she was done. Twilka put her hand to his forehead, avoiding contact with the tariqna tattoo.

"You're hot, maybe running a fever. If Nick and Mara don't arrive on schedule tomorrow, I'll have to get my hands on meds for you somehow."

"I'll be fine. If I could call upon the Lady, I'd have been healed already."

"Right, she's the answer to all your problems. Except when she's not. Or when she tries to kill you. But you persist in running back." The room featured only a bed and the bare essentials of a bathroom behind a sliding panel. After discarding the bloody towel in the bathroom, Twilka picked a spot further down the wall from where he lay on the bed, sat on the floor, and pulled out her AI, reviewing her designs to take her mind off the situation.

"Pretty," he said a few minutes later. "With an edge. They all remind me of you."

She whisked the designs out of view, into the file, and set the AI aside. "You're a fashion critic now?"

He held out one hand. "Sit with me? Please?"

"I don't think me and you on the bed is a good idea."

"Why not?"

"My damn body's forgotten you broke my heart." She rose to get the water bottle from her pack and brought it to him. "You should stay hydrated."

He caught her wrist, his fingers circling her arm like a bracelet. "We need to talk and I don't know how much time we have. The Brotherhood could find us before Nick arrives."

She tugged, but he wasn't going to let her go. Gracefully, she sank onto the edge of the bed, moving to sit cross-legged, facing him.

He released her and ran a hand over his face. "I didn't abandon you on Temple Home. Or at least not willingly."

Tilting her head, Twilka raised both eyebrows. "Seemed like it to me. Did I ever see you again? Did you even send word, say goodbye?"

"I couldn't." Leaning his head against the wall, he closed his eyes. "What do you remember of our final evening?"

"Drums. There we were in the White Lady's temple across the great square and your Lady had her people pounding the drums, for a ritual, you said. The sound echoed—it was eerie. The percussion symphony gave me a migraine, but you were restless, pacing, agitated. I went to bed and you left the room. And I never saw you again until the other night on the *Nebula Zephyr*."

"The drums were her heartbeat."

"Literally?"

"Yes. Only you and I could hear them. She was calling me to tazlin. I-I tried to resist, tried to remember she'd stripped me of my rank, my tariqna, tried to kill me. Finally, I decided to confront her, tell her I didn't want to re-enter the Brotherhood. Get the official separation over with. Being a prideful fool, I didn't want to accept the White Lady's help with handling the intricacies of detaching from her sister's service. And I didn't want to risk your entering my Lady's actual presence." Gaze intense, he stared at Twilka for a moment.

Sensing more behind the words than just a desire to spare her an encounter with the terrifying goddess, Twilka whispered her question, unsure if he'd answer. "Because?"

"I was going to tell her I wanted life with you. Refuse to accept reinstatement as a D'nvannae."

The answer, delivered in a flat tone, left her shaken for a moment. "What would have happened if I'd gone too?"

"She probably would have killed you. I don't know if the Lady in White would have intervened, since you had taken no vows, never belonged to the D'nvannae in any real sense. You merely touched the edge of *tazlin* once, on the *Dream,* through me."

"Yeah, once was enough." Of all the time spent trying to escape the wrecked *Nebula Dream,* that encounter stood out as a moment of bliss with Khevan, followed by sheer horror as the goddess took revenge. *I might have nightmares about the men in the corridor, but the Red Lady's malice was on a whole other level. Good thing I was unconscious for most of it.*

"Maybe the Lady in White was protecting you, if you only suffered a headache instead of the hypnotic lure. You had no desire to go to the source?"

"None." Twilka remembered the percussive sound that night on Temple Home had not only given her a huge migraine, it had set off a major anxiety attack. "All I wanted to do was hide. Or run."

There was silence for a few moments. Khevan shifted a bit, as if to seek a more comfortable position and was unable to do so. "Do we have more water?"

Twilka shook the bottle. "Empty." She rose and refilled the container in the tiny bathroom. When she brought the dripping container to him, she said, "I can sneak out later and get us food."

"Don't take the chance, not with the Brotherhood on the hunt." He drank avidly. "We won't starve in one night."

"Life on the run just gets better and better." Twilka took the bottle and set it on the floor. "So. Tell me the rest."

There was a moment of silence. Eyes closed, he said, "When you pledge your life to the Red Lady, when you become a D'nvannae, you swear terrible oaths, to serve her and preserve her secrets."

"Yeah, you told all of us that on the *Nebula Dream*. But you and I didn't get the chance to have *this* conversation, to clear the air about why we didn't work out." Tossing her hair, she made one of her self-protective flippant remarks. "The story of my life—I've never had a lasting relationship with a hot guy. Maybe I should stop blaming the Red Lady. Maybe the lack or failure is part of my own personality."

"I won't sit here and let you disrespect yourself," he said. He held out his hand. "There's nothing wrong with you."

She sat on the edge of the bed and scooted closer until their legs were touching. "So, talk."

"As part of the oath process, the applicant gives the Lady complete access to his mind. No mental blocks, no shielded areas. She can enter at any time. A Brother belongs to her, body and soul."

Twilka shivered, a wave of nausea passing through her gut. "Sounds awful."

"There are rewards." His smile was a bit crooked. "She doesn't normally exercise her rights or deploy the power against those who serve her. She has the entire hierarchy of the Brotherhood to enforce her will. When *tazlin* occurs, yes, we would also join mind to mind, but as you experienced, it's an intensely sensual experience, mutually…"

"Yeah, I get it." Twilka held up her hand. She had no intention of discussing her encounter involving the Red Lady any further.

Khevan returned to his narrative. "When I walked into the temple that night five years ago, drawn by the drums, she had eight brothers waiting for me. I fought, of course, but her men overpowered me through sheer force of numbers and brought me to her innermost sanctum, deep below the main temple. She demanded my oath again, as I'd willingly given it the first time, so many years ago. I refused. She roared into my mind like a hurricane of fire, scouring every corner, draining every memory and giving them back as pale shadows of what I'd lived, burning all my nerve endings. Mental and physical agony. Much worse than during the original oath ceremony, when she was a gracious goddess accepting an awestruck boy's pledge. This time she was angry at a man she felt had betrayed her."

Twilka slid her hand over his much larger one and squeezed gently. "Did it hurt?"

"Like being burned alive, from the inside out. I tried to fight her. I had one small blocked off area where I'd kept my memories of three things precious to me, to Khevan the man, not the D'nvannae Brother." He gave her a rueful smile. "My mother's people have a small gift of power, nothing to boast of, not like the Mellurean race commands, but we can accomplish a few things. Construct mind blocks on specific information or memories. The goddess didn't know what I'd hidden, but once she became aware of the secret, she wanted whatever it was as tribute, as payment for my rebellion."

He fell silent and Twilka didn't press for details. He'd tell her or he wouldn't. Her eyes filled with tears because they'd never talked at this level before. The way they'd met had been so intense, their connection so rushed, so charged with mutual sexual attraction, they'd never really gotten to know each other.

He touched her cheek with his knuckles, gently caressing. "What are you thinking? You drifted far away from me."

She swiped at her eyes. "Wishing we'd met in a more normal way than on a dying spaceship. I wish we'd had time to be friends first, before the disaster kicked in." She laid her head on his shoulder, taking his hand in hers. "We never had much of a chance, did we?"

He shifted against the pillows to put his arm around her. "Even if the *Nebula Dream* had completed her voyage intact, even if we'd slept together every night for the rest of the cruise, we probably wouldn't have connected heart to heart. We'd have gone our separate ways. It took the crucible of the night's events to break the walls."

"Harsh but true, I guess." She would have boasted to her 'Lite friends of the unusual conquest and moved on with them to the next party or event. And he would have taken on his subsequent contract and stayed a loyal soldier to his Lady. "We're a fluke, is what you're saying."

He tilted her chin and kissed her on the lips, gently at first, then seeking entry, his tongue probing at the seam. On a sigh, hesitating for only a heartbeat, she opened to him and lost herself in the moment, the sensations overwhelming. Khevan tasted so good, the warmth of him was so enticing, she couldn't resist. When the caress ended, she snuggled closer to him, being careful to avoid the bandaged wound.

"What memories did you keep from her in this mental lockbox?" she asked.

"My last happy memory of my mother before she died and my memory of the moment I chose which Lady to serve. As long as I had those pictures clearly in my mind, the chance of appealing to the Lady in White at some point remained. Or so I hoped. My mother had wanted me to go into the other Lady's service. She raised me on the stories of the glorious exploits of the Monks of Light, but after her death, my stepfather sold me to the Red Lady in exchange for enough credits to get his next fix of feelgoods."

"The Red Lady buys children?" Horror made it hard for Twilka to utter her question.

He nodded. "Only the ones with potential to be successful in either the Brotherhood or the Sisterhood. It's a better life than many would experience, left in the slums or on the streets. On many worlds having a child accepted into her temple service is a high aspiration, to be sought."

"Why don't the authorities put a stop to it? There can't be a treaty that allows her to recruit kids."

"You float in a rarefied atmosphere," he said, as if he was accusing her of something. "Your father's generational billions of credits give him gravity, provide your secure position in the higher orbits of the Sectors, enable you to take everything you have for granted. Most have to deal with the situation they're born into, on whatever planet that may be. The Sectors' authorities try hard, but they're stretched thin across the stars, and the war with the Mawreg takes much of their attention. The Red Lady is their valuable ally." He shrugged. "Local planetary authorities prioritize what matters to them. The tradition is centuries old, deeply ingrained when it comes to the D'nvannae. And some do come to her as adults."

At a loss for words, Twilka shook her head. "I must seem naïve to you. I just never thought about any of this before."

"Why should you? What would have ever brought the issue to your attention? But you asked about my memories and I was explaining. I was only a boy and so angry—at my mother for dying and abandoning me, at my stepfather for killing her and selling me; take your pick—I could only see hatred. The flames suited me then. I wanted to learn everything the Brotherhood trainers could teach me." He flicked a glance at her. "I was going to kill my stepfather someday."

"You're not just an assassin," she said, refusing to allow him to label himself in such a way. His selfless actions on the *Nebula Dream* after the wreck hadn't come from the soul of a killer.

"No, although I am exceedingly good at it." He studied her face, as if to gauge her reaction to his statement. "I've committed many murders in her service,

Twilka. Far more assassinations than good deeds or bodyguard assignments." He touched the tattoo on his cheek. "The higher levels of the Brotherhood kill; we rarely protect. She prefers the energy of conferring death. I earned every detail of this brand on my face, most with a sentient's life being the price."

"Did you kill your stepfather?"

Khevan's laugh was abrupt. "Ironically, he died of an overdose long before I could move against him."

Pondering that, Twilka slid her hand under the edge of his shirt and rubbed his back, noting how tense his muscles were, enjoying the feel of him under her palm. Returning to the earlier subject, she asked, "Why did you fight to keep those memories from the Red Lady?"

"I sensed right from the beginning, even as a young boy, I needed to keep a piece of myself private, use the mental pictures as a touchstone. Later, as I became a man, attracted her interest and personal attention, and understood far more about the weight of being a D'nvannae, I needed to remain myself in the deepest recesses of my soul. Not to be completely lost in her fires, as so many in her inner circle have been. Those men are the true D'nvannae of legend—implacable, infallible."

Counting on her fingers, Twilka said, "Your mother, the White Lady—you said three memories, so what else?"

"You. The first moment I saw you on the shuttle, going to the *Nebula Dream*. You were so carefree, so happy. My attraction to you was unsettling—immediate and fierce. Not like anything I'd ever felt before."

Playfully, she drifted her hand over his crotch, where an impressive erection was straining the leather pants. "So you wanted to take me to bed before you even knew me?"

Khevan captured her hand and kissed her palm. "No. And yes. I'd come from a particularly nasty job on Glideon, and you were the complete opposite of the life I was living. Beautiful, happy, and fresh…"

She had to swallow hard before she could speak. "I was a mess, a 'Lite mess. Flying on feelgoods. And you sure didn't show any signs of attraction. I even tried flirting with Nick at one point, later in the trip but before the wreck, at the casino, to make you jealous, with no result."

"I knew I had to keep my distance from you; the temptation was too strong." He gave her a rueful grin. "Forbidden fire of a completely different sort. Then Fate threw us together on the dying ship."

There was silence for a few moments. Then Twilka asked, "What happened on Temple Home? With the Lady after she took you prisoner?"

"She tortured me. I calculated later the punishment went on for over a year. I lost all sense of my body, of time. My mind floated untethered in an ocean of flames, surrounded by her, battered by her will, her unceasing demands. I-I can't remember clearly now, but eventually I broke and gave her my oath of servitude again. Anything to stop the pain—she got what she wanted."

Disturbed by the raw emotion she heard in his voice, Twilka raised his hand to her lips and kissed the knuckles gently before rubbing his hand on her cheek. "She's an alien being, ancient and powerful. She exerted a small portion of her power on me and I nearly died. I don't know how you fought her for a year. I can't imagine what you endured."

He gathered her close, arms like steel bands holding her tight. Twilka could hear his heartbeat under her ear, strong and steady. His enticing scent filled her senses, reminding her of their few but intense times of complete intimacy.

Resting his head on top of hers, his voice low, Khevan continued the story. "After breaking me and stealing my memories, when I'd renewed my oath to her, she returned my mind to my body, gave back the majority of my memories so I'd be myself, but created blank spaces where the special ones I surrendered had been. I think it was like a game to her, insignificant, so she didn't care if I had perfect recall of the complete set of events of the *Nebula Dream*, for example. She only wanted the memories I'd withheld from her, you know?"

Twilka nodded, both frightened by the Red Lady's casual exercise of her power and angry on his behalf. "And then?"

"She kept me imprisoned in the temple for another year, serving her slightest whim like a slave, while I was required to rebuild my combat skills under the close supervision of three D'nvannae Brothers who outranked me at the time. Those men were the only people who knew the truth of what she did to me, how she got me back in line." He paused. "All of them are dead now."

Trying to understand the significance of the information, she asked, "Did you kill them?"

"No. I think she did, because she didn't wish it to be known how close I'd come to escaping her, and what it took to enslave me again. Pride, you know?"

She nodded. The Lady struck her as an extremely conceited being. The deaths of a few devoted adherents to keep her secrets wouldn't matter.

"Eventually, she gave me a simple kill contract to carry out, then another and so forth, increasing the complexity of the assignments, analyzing my behavior until she was sure I'd regained my previous level of dedication and would honor my oath if sent out alone and unleashed. We had *tazlin* again, which was her final test of me, and I satisfied her." Brow furrowed, he leaned his head against the wall. "In some ways, that was the worst moment of all."

"And your special memories?"

"I relinquished them to her under the torture, one by one. I can't remember my mother's face, her voice, her perfume…I do remember her telling me stories when I was little, but there's no warmth to the memory, no love. I have no link to the Lady in White, no connection at all any longer. I fought the Red Lady hard on those two, so she'd be deceived about the existence of a third, the most precious of all to me." Using his enormous strength, he shifted Twilka onto his lap, straddling him and facing him. Holding her there with gentle pressure, he touched his forehead to hers as he whispered, "You."

Twilka slid her hands under his shirt, rubbing the bare skin of his back again, and kissed him, long and deep, while rocking her sensitive thinly clad crotch over the hard outline of his arousal. She nibbled at his earlobe and pressed a kiss to the sensitive skin below it. "Once she allowed you to move about freely, why didn't you at least send me a message?"

"I was tempted. Daily. Such an act would have been a violation of my oath," he said. "But from what I observed on the vids, you appeared happy, and I thought it better not to disturb you. Better for me and for you to assume our story was done."

Running her fingers through his thick hair, undoing the tight braid and setting the silky strands loose the way she preferred, Twilka did the math in her head. At the time Khevan was re-entering the world, she'd been in the midst of a public, fiery love affair with a trideo star, both of them using each other for publicity, as much as for the incredibly hot sex. Her fledgling company was benefitting from all the attention and he'd been up for a huge role. As soon as he was cast and filming began, the relationship ended, and he moved on to sleeping with his co-star.

Before she could say anything, Khevan went on.

"I feared the very thing we're in the midst of now, if I allowed the Red Lady to have the slightest inkling I still cared for you. But when I found us traveling together on the *Nebula Zephyr*, I calculated it might be safe for us to at least talk. Although, the moment I saw you, I wanted to do more, much more." Holding her gaze with his own, he slid his hand down her body, sensuously tracing her curves, until he was cupping her mound through her thin leggings. Twilka parted her legs to allow him access and shifted her hips to increase the pressure against his hand. "But now I'm sure the whole thing was a setup on her part, an additional aspect of the test she was going to put me through."

Twilka tilted her head back, the better to see his face. "You're failing, my friend."

He kissed her throat. "I congratulated myself I was doing rather well." As he took her lips again, he slid one hand under the edge of her top and cupped her breast, massaging the nipple into a hard bud. She felt his rock hard erection pulse and strain more urgently against the leather pants.

"Depends who's judging." Raising her head from the kiss, she played with his earlobe, biting it gently before whispering, "What about your wound?"

A gleam came into his eyes and his lips quirked in a teasing smile. "I have a high pain threshold and the slash is mending rapidly. If we're careful…"

"All right then." She kissed him, thrusting her tongue into the warmth of his mouth, while busy working on the fastening of his pants. His cock sprang free and she locked her hand around the girth, massaging from root to tip. "I think we need fewer clothes."

He tugged at the hem of her shirt and, obligingly, she raised her arms so he could slide the garment over her head and toss it to the floor. Khevan stared hungrily at her for a moment, so she arched her back and, as if he couldn't stop himself, he cupped both breasts, teasing her nipples lightly with his thumb. He rolled her over on her back and moved on top of her, grimacing slightly as he adjusted his weight and the bandage over his injury pulled taut.

"I missed you," he said softly, brushing a strand of her tousled hair off her face.

Twilka wriggled a bit, to allow his heavy cock to fall between her legs, nudging at the fabric blocking the entrance to her body. "Still too many damn clothes. Let me up for a moment so I can take off my leggings. And your pants."

When she'd stripped them both naked, she sank back onto the bed and pulled him on top of her. With a sigh, she shifted her hips, allowing the tip of his erection to slide between her slick folds. "Hard and fast," she said, hands cupping his butt. "That's how badly I want you right now. We can do foreplay later—we have the entire night ahead of us."

"Never are you a patient woman and especially not in bed." He laughed, thrusting his powerful hips to drive further inside her. "You'll get no argument from me. It's been too long since I had you wrapped around me. There's been no other woman for me since that night I left you on Temple Home."

Twilka stilled as a frightening thought occurred to her. "But you've been with the goddess in *tazlin*. Will she be able to find us? To appear like she did before?"

Raising himself on his elbows, he said, "It's always possible, but I don't feel her presence. To project herself so far across the Sectors is a drain on her energy; that's why she had to be lured with *tazlin* rituals when we were on the *Nebula*

Dream. I'd never expose you to the risk of her intruding here. Nothing between us here and now is tainted with *tazlin*; I give you my word. It's just us in this bed."

"Together, the way we're meant to be," she said with a sigh of satisfaction, tilting her hips and wrapping her legs around him to drive him deeper into her aching core. "I've missed you."

As he flexed his body, thrusting and nearly withdrawing, only to push further into places within that had been too empty for too long, she found the right rhythm, craving the release only he could give her. It was if no time had passed since the last time they made love. Her body was tight around him, his girth and length filling her to the satisfaction of every nerve ending. The delicious tremors of orgasm spread outward from her core and she clung tighter to him as he reached his climax a moment later, holding her as if for dear life itself.

They lay together sated, bodies as closely entwined as two humans can be.

"Now it's your turn to be patient," he whispered, stroking her hair away from her face. "Give me but a few minutes, and then we'll begin again, and take our time, all right? I want to pleasure you properly."

"Trust me, you achieved that goal, but I'm not opposed to more." She laughed, running her hand down his chest and abdomen, to where their bodies were still joined, finding him already more than a little aroused. It pleased her that she had such an effect on him. "If all we have is this one night," she said, staring into his eyes, "I want to make it so memorable that the Red Lady couldn't erase the moments no matter what she did to us."

"Beloved, we've already accomplished that." He kissed her softly. "But we can and will embellish upon the excellent beginning."

CHAPTER FIVE

In the morning, she dressed and went out to find food for them, over his protests. "You're too recognizable, you said so yourself," she told him. "I'm just a down on her luck woman of no special significance." She gestured at her clothes. "These weren't high fashion to begin with and now, after yesterday mingling with the crowds in the bazaar, a grease stain or two from the bad food we've been eating, and tearing strips off the shirt to make you a bandage, I look even more disreputable. I'll fit right in on the street. There are at least five different automated fast food stalls close by." She held out her hand. "Give me the credits and shut up."

"So commanding." He dug the requested funds from the pocket of his discarded pants and handed them over, clasping her wrist as he did so, holding her in place. "Be careful. Please."

Twilka gazed into his eyes. "I promise. But we have to have food. You may be healing faster than a normal person would, but your body needs energy." Heat bloomed in her cheeks. "Especially after the way we spent the night."

"Don't be gone long." He rose, grabbing his pants and getting dressed.

Twilka slipped out the hotel's rear exit and picked her way through a garbage-strewn alley to connect with the main street. She kept her head tucked and her hands in her pockets, shivering against the morning chill. It was a work day on this world and even in the slum men and women were hurrying to their jobs. She mingled with the crowd and passed up the closest eatery vendor, drifting along in the wake of a group of women roughly her age. Although she didn't see police or any sign of the Brotherhood, the back of her neck tingled and she was tense as she bought breakfast sandwiches and cups of synthcaff, using nearly all the credits. About to leave the shop to set foot on the sidewalk, she froze as two D'nvannae walked past, constantly scanning the crowd. Twilka retreated a step, earning herself a shove from the impatient person behind her. Juggling the two cups of synthcaff, she emerged from the eatery, strolling casually in the direction the D'nvannae had gone, but staying well back. The Brothers were using a handheld tracking device and paused for a moment in front of the hotel, heads together, studying the readout.

She stopped to stare at the flickering holos in a dingy store window as one Brother glanced at his surroundings, as if searching for someone. Studying them in the faint reflection on the streaked window, she thought their tattoos were intricate but nowhere near as high level as Khevan's. *Are they from Temple Home or local talent?*

When the man swiveled his head to scrutinize the immediate vicinity, Twilka traveled in the other direction, making a turn at the corner, handing one synthcaff to an old man begging beside an empty store, slurping the other awkwardly as she ran, sack of food clutched in her free hand. She ducked into the rear entrance of the hotel and scrambled up the old fashioned staircase, glad she had such strong leg muscles from all her years of avoiding gravlifts. Her hand was trembling as she tried to activate the door to their room, but after two tries she was inside.

The portal slammed shut and she leaned against the panel, her chest heaving. Khevan stared at her. "I gather we're in trouble?"

She tossed him the food bag. "D'nvannae right outside the hotel. They didn't see me. We've got to go before they surround the place, so eat fast."

"How many?" He extracted the greasy meatroll from the container and wolfed it down in three bites.

She handed him the dregs of the synthcaff. "Two, equipped with a high tech tracking device in the Red Lady's trademark scarlet finish. If they've trailed us here, they'll be able to pinpoint the room, right? How the seven hells are they following you?"

"All D'nvannae carry a trace element of the Lady's essence in their blood. An unfortunate side effect of the oath ceremony. I was hoping this rural temple wouldn't have access to the sophisticated technology, although I did sweep our hotel room yesterday when we left, to nullify the traceability just in case. But I can be tracked in the open as well, if the operator knows what he or she is doing. The Lady keeps this a secret and severely limits the number of such scanners for obvious reasons."

"So these guys must be from Temple Home then."

"Most likely." He was on his feet. "The compliance squad."

"Can you do the invisibility thing? Can *they* see you?"

He paused. "I can only maintain it for a brief time, but no, the brothers wouldn't be able to penetrate the cloaking. What do you have in mind?"

"Let's go out the back and you stay invisible as long as you can. I've already been in their vicinity out on the street and no one noticed me, so maybe my disguise is good enough. You must be their primary target. We need to get out of this area and get to the spaceport. Nick is arriving any time now—he might even be on the planet already."

Shrugging into his jacket after a cursory look under the bandage at his knife wound, he said, "You're putting a lot of faith in our old friend."

"You bet I am. He worked miracles getting us off the *Nebula Dream* alive."

Khevan nodded. "I can't deny the truth."

"And he does have the ability to ask the Mellureans for help—the Red Lady has to listen to them, everyone in the Sectors does."

"The Brothers know we're here, pointless to sweep the room clean now," Khevan said. "Ready to go?"

"No, but we'd better move." She swallowed hard and tried to calm her hammering pulse. This could become a walking nightmare if the D'nvannae were waiting in the corridor.

She emerged on Khevan's heels, relieved to find the hall empty, and hastened to the stairs, Khevan in front. Twilka's nerves were ragged as she made a rapid descent to the ground floor and the rear entrance she'd used moments earlier. "Let me go first," she said. "I'll check the alley. Then you can do your handy trick and join me if the coast is clear. I'll head left at the end of the street and we'll go east from there, toward the spaceport."

"West. We'll lay a false trail, as if we might be headed to the White Lady's temple, useless though it would be. Then we can double back toward the spaceport."

Hand on the door access, she said, "Sounds good." Opening the portal, she stepped confidently into the alley, forcing herself to keep moving when she found a D'nvannae Brother waiting there, trying to act as if his presence had no significance to her. Head down, she kept close to the wall and scurried a few steps.

A groundcar pulled up, blocking the end of the alley. She faltered, then continued in that direction anyway. What else was there to do?

"Twilka Zabour?"

Ignoring the man, she walked faster.

He grabbed her by the elbow, a grip she couldn't break. Dragging her into the center of the alley, blaster in his other hand, the Brother said, "I'll kill her now, Khevan, if you don't show yourself. I know you're here."

"No!" Twilka screamed and launched herself at her captor, trying to punch and kick him.

Laughing, the man handed her off to another D'nvannae who'd come up behind them. "Hold this wildcat for me while I deal with the traitor."

As she was forced to her knees on the damp pavement with a blaster aimed at her head, Twilka watched Khevan shed his invisibility. Four of the Brotherhood surrounded him, shoving him against the wall, hands raised.

"Let her go, Harbin," Khevan said, as the men disarmed him, not missing a single visible or hidden weapon on his person. "This is between the Lady and me; the woman's not truly involved."

Head tilted, the leader studied him for a moment, before pivoting on his heel and assessing Twilka. "She's got a kill contract on her head. I'd say she's involved." He walked to where Twilka knelt and grabbed her by the hair, examining her face. "Not very impressive. Certainly not enough to inspire a man like you to try to thwart the Lady," he said to Khevan over his shoulder. "I expected more." He leaned closer, staring into Twilka's eyes now. "You don't resemble your holographs without all the façade of complicated makeup. Disappointing."

She surged upward, trying to bite him, head butt him, take action to express her defiance, no matter how ineffective, but Harbin stepped adroitly away and the other brother seized her, shoving her into the submissive pose on her knees again.

"She does have pale fire," Harbin said. "A flicker." He strolled to where Khevan knelt, hands behind his head. "You were foolish to accept the last assignment with the archaeological expedition and leave Temple Home. One might almost think you wanted to keep your distance from our beloved and benevolent goddess. The Lady was lonely and there I was, ready to step in."

So this was all about Temple politics. Twilka studied the men surrounding her. The six Brothers had detailed tariqnas. High ranking, with Harbin being maybe a shade below Khevan, judging by the complexity of his tattoo.

"Only so many places at the Red Lady's table, only so many spots for upholding the duties of *tazlin*," Harbin said, while she was evaluating the caliber of the men confronting them. "I might not have dared to move had you been there, or perhaps I'd have taken steps against one of the others at your rarefied level, but since you were conveniently absent, and remain a bit tainted from your earlier desertion, I seized my chance for advancement. I whispered doubt into her ear, subtle comments when the opportunities presented themselves, eventually suggested a test of faith and loyalty to resolve the uncertainty I'd created."

"You talk too much," Khevan said. "If you have to tell me how brilliant you are…"

Harbin spun on his heel to glance at Twilka. "The Lady remembered *you* and not fondly, which helped my cause."

Clenching her jaw, Twilka said, "Not one of my better memories either. Your Lady is a bitch."

Quicker than a cat, Harbin was at her side again, raising his arm to deliver a blow which sent Twilka spinning to the trash-strewn pavement. He stood over her, nudging her none too gently in the ribs with the toe of his boot. "Speak with disrespect of the Lady again and you'll suffer more pain before I enforce the kill order."

Wondering if her jaw was broken, dizzy from the blow and the impact when her head hit the street, Twilka enunciated as clearly as she could. "Fuck her. And you."

Attempting to intervene, Khevan fought his captors. "Leave her alone. Your quarrel is with me."

"Your turn will come." Harbin flicked his fingers at the guard, who pulled Twilka upright, the rough handling increasing her dizziness. He drew his ruby-handled knife and stepped closer. "A moment's indulgence, Brother Khevan, while I carry out the assignment given to you. Watch and learn."

"Preexisting contract of protection, never revoked or cancelled," Khevan shouted. "By the Lady's own law you can't kill this woman."

Confused, Twilka stared at him.

Harbin toyed with the knife, running the blade along her cheek, not breaking the skin, and lifting one curl of her hair in an obscene parody of a caress. "No such contract is registered. Are you adding perjury to your crimes?"

"A Brother may contract for service personally and render the payment to the treasury later," Khevan said.

"Do you have proof?"

Khevan shifted his arms fractionally and in a heartbeat the four men surrounding him had their scarlet blasters aimed at his head. Raising his empty hands high in the air, he said, "I give you my word; I'm only reaching for the proof you've requested."

"Let him play this charade out. If he attempts treachery, shoot to stun." Harbin appeared unconcerned by any resistance Khevan might undertake.

The three D'nvannae shifted to allow Khevan space, blasters still at the ready. Khevan opened the small pouch at his belt and withdrew something too small for Twilka to see, not to mention the fact her vision was blurred at the moment. Another man took the item from Khevan and handed it to the waiting Harbin. He took a small scanner tipped with a glinting ruby from his vest pocket and ran it over his palm, where the offering lay. There was a flare of red light, tiny but unmistakable. Twilka thought Khevan sagged, as if in relief.

But we never agreed to a contract. I didn't pay him anything to seal such a bond, not now, not five years ago. She bit her lip to keep from saying anything out loud.

Khevan frowned at her, reinforcing the concept that this was the time to remain silent.

"Release her," Harbin said with a casual wave of the hand. "Antecedent protective contract verified, nullifying the current kill contract, both now hereby cancelled and void." He flipped the token in her direction and, reflexively, Twilka reached to catch it. "Lucky happenstance for you." Pointing the knife at her, he said, "You're free to go. Stay under the scanners and the Lady may forget about you, once she's finished with him. *I* certainly don't care if you live or die. You have no value once he's neutralized."

Rising to her feet with difficulty as the Brother behind her backed away, she said, "What will happen to Khevan?"

"None of your concern." Harbin issued orders to his men. "Lock him in the restraints. We've wasted enough time here. Only one thing left to do and we can be on our way home as the Lady commands."

Eyes locked on her, Khevan offered no resistance as his arms were cuffed behind him.

Harbin drew his knife and stood beside his prisoner, hand grasping Khevan's braid, pulling his head back so his neck was exposed.

"No!" Twilka screamed and took a step, stumbling and falling to her knees.

"He's disgraced," Harbin said. "But never fear, I'm not planning to kill him while you watch. His fate is at the whim of the Lady and she wishes to enjoy each protracted moment of his death." He hacked at Khevan's black hair, severing the tightly braided queue and tossing it to the ground. Sliding the knife into its sheath, he took the blaster from the nearest brother and burned the hair into ash. "Put him in the groundcar."

Giving her one last glance, as if trying to memorize her face, Khevan allowed himself to be wrestled away to the waiting vehicle.

"I wish I could say it's been a pleasure, but sadly, it wasn't." Harbin's tone was chiding.

"You'll pay for this," she said wildly, wiping blood from her split lip.

"No, I won't. On the contrary, the Lady stands ready to reward me richly for besting your former lover in our little temple games. Pray we never meet again, Twilka Zabour. I won't spare you twice." Turning on his heel, he walked to a second car which had pulled up behind the first. A moment later, Twilka was choking on the fumes as the procession sped off.

She pulled herself to the small platform at the hotel's back door and sat for a moment. Slowly uncurling her hand, she realized she held a small golden charm in the shape of a combined star and moon. Instinctively she put a hand to her neck, where the trinket had once been part of an elaborate, many stranded necklace, a one of a kind designer original. *But when I tried to contract with him on the* Nebula Dream, *to give him the jewelry as payment to get me to safety, he refused. And then the pirates stole the necklace…when did he take this?* Her vision wavered and she realized people were beginning to venture into the alley, encroaching on her personal space. Hastily, she stowed the precious charm in her pocket and got to her feet, swaying precariously. Hunched against the pain in her head and jaw, she staggered out of the lane, heading east in line with her original plan, toward the spaceport. Moving as fast as she could, she put distance between herself and the spot where Khevan had been taken.

No one followed her, for which she was grateful. She figured she looked so unattractive by now, dirty, disheveled and bleeding, people would give her a wide berth. She had to stop frequently to rest, leaning on the wall of whatever building was closest. Twilka overheard disdainful comments made by passersby, assuming she was high on feelgoods. Once she felt she'd gone far enough for it to be safe, she ducked into an access driveway and took out her personal AI. Punching in the code for Nick Jameson took three shaky tries. While she waited for the connection to open, she closed her eyes and slid down the rough wall, sitting on the damp ground.

"What the seven hells happened to you?" Nick was staring at her in the vid.

"Nice to see you again too, soldier."

"Where are you? Where's Khevan?"

"Gone. The Brotherhood took him. I don't know where I am." She swallowed, the flat metallic taste of blood in her throat. "I think I'm going to be sick or pass out, or both."

"Leave the link open so I can home in on you. I see you're close to the spaceport. I'll be there in ten minutes or less." Eyes narrowed, he leaned closer in the vid. "Stay awake, Twilka; promise me you won't go to sleep."

"I promise." She could barely form the words. The pain in her head was hot, blinding her, and her jaw ached when she talked. She tucked the AI into her pocket and concentrated on staying conscious. Nick was coming. He and Mara would make everything all right.

At first she feared she'd returned to her nightmare. Feebly she struck out, hands fisted.

"Stand down; it's me." Nick was bending over her, lifting her carefully into his arms. "Someone did a number on you, kid."

"We have to get her to the hospital," Mara said, peering over his shoulder, face set in a worried expression.

"No hospital." She enunciated as clearly as she could, not moving her head after the first flare of pain. "Too many questions asked. Bad for my image to look so terrible in public. That was a joke, by the way."

"If you can crack jokes, you'll live." Nick carried her effortlessly to the waiting groundcar. "Compromise then. We have an excellent sickbay on our ship. We'll get Casey to check you out and if he says you have to go to the hospital, no more arguments. You remember Casey?"

The name pulled up memories. Everything connected with the night of the wreck was crystal in her mind, even now, injured as she was. "On the *Space Dragon*, yeah."

Mara slid into the back seat of the ground car and held out her arms to help get Twilka into the car with a minimum of jostling, as if she was a child. Nick gently deposited Twilka next to her, while the car dipped as another person climbed in on the other side. Whoever was in the driver's seat gunned the engine as Nick shut the passenger door. He'd come with reinforcements.

"What happened?" Mara asked, as she put her arm around Twilka.

She laid her head on Mara's comforting shoulder and closed her eyes, trying not to cry. "The Brotherhood caught up to us. They were going to kill me. The guy in charge, Harbin, didn't like the way I talked about their Lady." Twilka laughed despite the pain, as she remembered the horror on his face at her insulting words. "She is a bitch, though. No one knows better than me."

"I'll be most curious why he didn't carry out the contract," said the passenger on the other side of Mara. Twilka didn't recognize the voice and her eyes weren't cooperating. "Unprecedented," the man added, his voice deep, with a rasp.

"You can ask her later." Mara was firm, patting Twilka's arm. "Save your strength, sweetie."

The ground car slid to a smooth halt. She didn't remember anything of the drive through the city and onto the spaceport. *I must have passed out.*

Nick carried her from the car to the *Space Dragon* in her berth at the spaceport, going straight to sickbay once he cleared the onramp. "I could get spoiled by this treatment, soldier," she said, attempting another joke. "Maybe I should hire you to keep my feet from touching the ground ever again."

"I don't think Mara would approve," he said. "And I'd get bored, hate to tell you. No offense."

"None taken. I remember this place," she said, as he laid her on the examining table in the *Space Dragon's* sickbay. "You carried me in here the first time too."

"We've enhanced the fittings a bit. You don't look so good, lady." Red haired, big as a house, unforgettable Sgt. Casey approached her with a medscanner.

"Nice to see you too," she said. "Got anything to eat on this ship?"

"Later." He frowned. "Let me see what you've got going on in that head of yours first." He made a pushing motion with his other arm. "If I could have room to work here, please."

"I'll stay," Mara told whoever else was crowding the space.

"Call me if you need anything." Nick bent over the table, coming into Twilka's blurry field of vision. "You're safe now; no one's going to know you're here with us until you give the word. And no one's going to hurt you again, soldier's oath. They'll have to go through me first."

She held up her hand and he squeezed it carefully. "Thank you," she whispered. Casey gave her an inject in the opposite arm and the world shrank to a pinpoint and went away.

CHAPTER SIX

Despite her anxiety for Khevan, it was the next day before she could stay awake and felt well enough to get dressed in clothing borrowed from Mara and attend an informal council of war in the *Space Dragon's* dining hall. Nick brought her a mug of genuine coffee, setting it in front of her with a flourish and going to sit beside Mara, one arm casually looped over the back of her chair, rubbing his wife's shoulder. "Glad you've regained your energy. You were pretty bedraggled when we brought you in."

"I think you must have an illegal rejuve resonator in your sickbay," she said, sipping at the coffee. "I feel so much improved."

Nick and Mara exchanged glances, but neither confirmed nor denied her remark.

"Hey, you had a great medic; admit it." Casey laughed as he and Rafferty ambled into the room. "I can cook too." He set a plate of scrambled eggs, hashed tubers, and two kinds of toast in front of Twilka before going to sit beside Raff.

She realized she was starving and picked up her fork to sample the eggs.

"I know you need to eat real food versus the nutrient packs we gave you last night, so take your time, but we're eager to hear what happened," Mara said.

Twilka stared at the last person who arrived for the conversation. He had the unmistakable demeanor of a D'nvannae Brother, muscular, quiet as a cat, dressed in head to toe black leather, but exhibiting no scarlet tariqna tattoo or other sign of allegiance to the Lady. His long blond hair was caught in a casual ponytail, not braided or loose. She had to exert all her willpower not to shrink away from him as he took a chair, although he made no hostile move. "I'm sorry, I don't know you," she said, pointing her fork at him accusingly.

"Where are my manners?" Nick spoke up promptly. "This is a special consultant I brought in, given the nature of your problem, as I understood the message. Twilka Zabour, meet Quaid Jacq, or as he's more commonly known in our overlapping circles of business, the Renegade. Lucky for us, he was available."

Quaid bowed his head to her and shook her hand.

Twilka studied him again, head to toe. Something wasn't adding up. "I-I don't understand. I thought you were a D'nvannae Brother, the way you carry yourself, the way you move…"

"I am," he said.

She looked at Nick for reassurance. He nodded. "Highest ranking D'nvannae alive. But not to worry, he doesn't serve the Lady any longer."

"She and I came to a parting of the ways," Quaid said.

"Then you're *not* a Brother?" Her head was whirling and she didn't appreciate the mystery Nick and this newcomer were presenting to her.

"It suits us both to keep my name on the rolls of the order. I have access to certain resources, can exercise useful privileges without accepting orders or commands. I don't report to the goddess, if you're concerned. I'm free to pursue anything I find interesting, even if the matter puts me into direct opposition to her goals. Hence the Renegade nickname."

Still suspicious, Twilka spread lavender seedless whelgra jam on her toast. "What does she get out of it?"

"I have something she wants and refuse to give to her. She can't take it by force; she can't find it anywhere else—we have a standoff." He regarded her for a moment, brilliant blue eyes measuring. "You're not the one to whom I must reveal this secret. It won't help or hinder you."

"I don't care about your secrets if they don't concern Khevan." Twilka rubbed her forehead. "I don't really understand, but if you think he can help us, Nick, I'll take your word for it."

"Okay, introductions over," Mara said, not a hair out of place, taking charge as if she'd assembled the group for a routine business meeting. "Why don't you fill us in on the situation, Twilka?"

She swallowed her bite of toast, enjoying the tang of the jam. "First of all, thank you for coming. I should have said that earlier, I know. Khevan and I didn't know what to do, where to turn when he got the kill contract on me, and realized the Lady herself had issued it."

"Yet he refused to honor it?" Quaid leaned forward, eyes narrowed.

"Let her tell us in her own way," Mara ordered.

In between bites of egg and toast, with sips of coffee to wash the meal down, Twilka recited the events since the night Khevan had appeared in her hotel room, leaving out the lovemaking interlude in the second fleabag hotel. "And then today, when we left the robohotel to come meet you, the D'nvannae were waiting, jumped us. Khevan surrendered when he saw they were going to hurt me if he didn't. Harbin confirmed this entire setup with the kill contract and the compliance squad was all about temple politics—the man's a douche and he talks too much, but I guess he outmaneuvered Khevan pretty badly."

"Or for some reason, old times perhaps, you caused Khevan to make missteps," Quaid said. "Starting with his refusal to kill you."

"Fair enough." Twilka acknowledged the point.

"And now we come to the point where I'm keenly interested to know how you prevented your own death at Harbin's hands?"

"Khevan said there was a previous protection contract still in effect and I couldn't be killed."

"What proof did he offer?"

Twilka fumbled in her pocket and withdrew the golden charm, holding it out in her hand. "This."

The others leaned closer to see. Mara gasped. "I remember that necklace! But he refused your contract offer. I was so angry you'd even tried to get his services exclusively…"

"I wasn't thinking clearly at that point," Twilka said. "I would have asked him to help all of us, of course, but I wanted the security of his promise to me as a D'nvannae. I was so scared."

"Space dust under the jets now," Nick said. "We all know how it turned out and each of us had our part to play." He glanced at Rafferty and Casey, sitting quietly at the end of the table. "Including you guys." Raff raised his coffee mug to acknowledge the remark.

"And Harbin accepted this?" Quaid asked.

"He did a test on it, there was a red spark when he ran the scanner over it and he was satisfied. He told me both contracts were terminated now." Twilka replaced the charm in her pocket. "Honestly, I don't know when Khevan took the token, maybe when we were descending the *Dream's* gravlift together. I didn't have a contract with him, to my knowledge."

"Apparently, the Brother believed he did, in his heart." Quaid's voice was firm. "From what I've heard here, you asked and he took payment. The fact you were unaware of the contract until yesterday is odd, but not a deal breaker."

"But the kill order is cancelled?" Mara asked.

Twilka nodded, sipping her coffee, enjoying the warmth as the stimulant hit her system.

"Harbin wouldn't have left her alive otherwise." Quaid sounded sure.

"Dead in an alley with my throat cut," she said, shivering at the realization of her close call. *Maybe I'll have a new nightmare now.*

"How did Khevan hide that token from the goddess, if he was a prisoner for a year or so?" Rafferty asked.

Twilka shrugged. "Maybe no one searched his things? I don't know—Khevan has his ways."

"The Lady wouldn't care about his clothing or personal effects," the Renegade said. "Not if she was as angry with him as you've said. She'd go straight for his mind, his soul, you might term it, in order to break him down and impose her will again. Then when he was reinstated, his quarters and possessions would have been returned to him as a matter of course. He stood high in the ranks."

"So the real question is, what do you want to do next?" Nick toyed with his empty coffee mug, making it spin on the table, and regarded Twilka with raised eyebrows.

"What do you mean?"

"Your life isn't in jeopardy any longer. We can drop you off at your hotel, you can pick up where you left off…"

"Are you crazy?" She jumped from her chair as if ready to leave immediately. Dizziness assaulted her and she grabbed the top rim of the seat to steady herself. "We have to go help Khevan before the goddess kills him. I'm not leaving him in her hands. I'm not abandoning him."

"He walked away from you five years ago," Mara said, drawing a pattern on the table with her spoon.

"No. He explained what happened." Twilka glanced from face to face, trying to convince them. "The Red Lady set a trap for him and then she kept him in a kind of mental prison for a year, trying to brainwash him." She appealed to Quaid, placing her hand on his arm tentatively. "You must know—you were just talking about what she does."

"She has her ways of reclaiming errant Brothers," he said. "Moving on to a more relevant issue today, it's rare, although not impossible, for a man to leave the D'nvannae order. At the higher levels which Khevan achieved, separation is unheard of. Not without a special advantage, such as I hold, to force her hand and obtain his release. I only remain a D'nvannae named on the rolls by mutual agreement, and I can rescind my status any time. I can walk away. Someone like your Khevan wouldn't have this option."

"Her sister, the White Lady, was going to help us after the wreck, or so we believed, but then he fell into the trap on Temple Home and we missed our chance to see her. Would she help him now?" Twilka asked Quaid, figuring he was her most likely source of information.

Shaking his head, he said, "No. Extremely unlikely. You had an unusual window of opportunity after surviving the wreck, which closed when he made his choice to stay in the flames."

"The Red Lady forced him."

"He hasn't asked us for help for himself," Nick said. He raised a hand as Twilka opened her mouth to protest. "Merely pointing out a fact. That doesn't mean I'm not willing to assume he needs it. I'm ready to go to Temple Home; you just say the word. But what makes you so sure he wants to leave the Brotherhood now?"

She felt a tear slip down her cheek followed by another as she edged back into the chair. "He loves me. He stayed in the Brotherhood to save my life by convincing the Lady I meant nothing to him anymore. He promised me we'd find a way to escape the Red Lady together this time. He's done serving her. He wants a life of his own, with me."

Mara left her chair, coming to hug Twilka. "We believe you. We'll figure something out. Nick's good at strategizing on the fly, you know that." She shot Nick a look.

"Find out if they've left the planet yet," Nick said to Rafferty. As the captain left the mess, Nick eyed Quaid. "What's the worst scenario here? Will she execute him?"

"She prefers to think of it as permanently absorbing the Brother into the flames," the Renegade said. "He'd be dead already if her anger was hot. She may be hoping to ensnare him again, might give him a chance to best Harbin, clean the slate as it were. Resume his place in *tazlin* with her. But if Khevan has decided to leave the Brotherhood and refuses her, she'll either kill him or she could subject him to *merdamier,* a sort of test, a trial. It's one of her few laws—any who requests to leave may try. I believe this ritual may be left over from whatever world her kind originated on. She clings to a few of her original tenets, regards them as unbreakable. Almost holy. Which is why Twilka survives today—because the Lady won't break her word and if a contract is agreed to in her name by a sworn member of the Order, she honors it."

"How many succeed in walking away?" Mara asked shrewdly.

Expressionless, Quaid raised his coffee mug. "None, to my knowledge, not in centuries."

Nick rolled his shoulders. "We need a plan. Can we break him out of the temple?"

Quaid shook his head. "Unlikely, without the White Lady or the Mellureans on our side."

"No help from the latter," Nick said, dashing Twilka's hopes as quickly as they were raised. "I asked my contacts for advice or intervention when I first got Twilka's message, and was politely declined. The Mellureans indicated things would work themselves out, which I guess the situation did, for Twilka anyway." He shot her a glance.

"I had no reason to expect them to step in on my behalf. They've got bigger issues to handle than my fate." She made herself smile with an effort. "Even I'm not *that* conceited."

"I think the Mellureans and the two Ladies try not to step on each other's toes, as much as possible," Mara said, giving her a hug. "Or maybe their answer to Nick was a prophecy and they felt it was enough help. Receiving a Mellurean prophecy is a dream realized because, good or bad, they always come true."

Nick drummed his fingers on the table for a moment. "I owe Khevan and I gave my solemn oath to come to his aid at any time, although for a guy like me it's easier if blasters and force are involved. This mystical stuff, the flames…" He shrugged and grinned. "Not my area, which is why I called Quaid in on this. I'm willing to accept Twilka's word Khevan wants out of the Brotherhood. I vote we go to Temple Home and see what can be done. Who's in?"

"Of course," Mara said, as if there couldn't be any question.

Casey cleared his throat. "We go where you need us, so I'll speak for Rafferty and me. The *Space Dragon* is at your disposal."

Twilka studied Quaid's expressionless face. "And you? If it's a question of credits…"

He held up his hand. "Nick hired me to help resolve the situation and as far as I can see, the job is only half done. I find myself taking an interest, sight unseen, in this Brother who wishes to extricate himself from the flames for a human woman. Consider me your ambassador to the Lady." Addressing Nick, he said, "I'll take my ship to Temple Home and see what I can find out. When you arrive, we'll talk about the best course of action based on what I've learned."

"You're sure a midnight extraction mission won't work? You could give us the layout of the place, diagram the vulnerabilities." Nick arched one eyebrow.

"If only rescuing him were so easy. You're the man to accomplish it. But I believe we want to end this without any more kill contracts, so a different approach will be needed." The Renegade looked at each person at the table in turn. "I can't predict right now what may be demanded of each of you, if we're to bring this Khevan out of the Lady's fire as a whole man. It may not be possible. It won't be simple, but the challenge intrigues me. And I only take on the jobs guaranteed to relieve my boredom. I'll see you when you arrive." He bowed to Twilka and then to Mara and was gone.

"You trust him?" she asked Nick.

"He's highly recommended, highly selective about the assignments he'll accept. I've worked with him once or twice. We're damn lucky he was available and willing to talk to us." Nick squeezed her shoulder as he walked past to get himself a second cup of coffee. "He's probably the only man alive who knows anything about the Red Lady's order and will talk about it."

"I'll be happy to reimburse you for his fee. If I don't have enough credits, I can ask my father for a loan on the business…" She struck herself in the forehead lightly. "Speaking of which, if I want to have a business, I'd better call my associates, let them know I'm fine. See how much damage my disappearance from the party did."

"There's been nothing on the news," Mara said. "I've been monitoring the major broadcasts and gossip feeds. The people who work for you must have decided discretion was the best tactic."

"I have a good team." A small rush of pride flooded Twilka's mind over the staff selections she'd made. Lissa was top notch, could probably run the entire business on her own, and Jord had finely honed deal making skills. *If we save Khevan, I could step away from all of it, let them run the company, maybe just do the designing and a few appearances.* Admonishing herself not to think too far ahead, she sipped her coffee. Nick and Mara had provisioned the *Space Dragon's* mess with the pure, Terran blend, which she knew for a fact cost pound for pound about as much as a small spaceship, if it could be obtained at all. The Sectors' military had first priority. Either the Jamesons' combined freight and security businesses were doing exceedingly well, or Mara was working decidedly unofficial contacts. Or both.

Rafferty re-entered the mess. "The D'nvannae ship cleared the atmosphere an hour ago. Are we following?"

"That's the plan," Nick said. "Set course for Temple Home. If you want to talk to your people, Twilka, do it before we hit hyperdrive."

The flight to Temple Home was uneventful and felt unbearably long to Twilka. She tried to lose herself in designing, but kept drawing Khevan's face. Nick and especially Mara did their best to distract her, but the truth was none of them had any idea what awaited them on Temple Home.

"I wish we'd asked the Renegade more about what we'd have to do to rescue Khevan," she said one evening at dinner.

"He might not know until he learns more at the central temple," Nick said reasonably.

"So, do you use the *Space Dragon* as your private ship now?"

He laughed. "Wish I could afford the luxury. The security business is doing well, but I'm not as rich as a generational billionaire yet. No, Rafferty and Casey agreed to help out with this one for old time's sake. I figured we'd need all the firepower we could get to take on the Red Lady."

"They do a lot of shipping runs for me," Mara said. "I promised they'd never be at a loss for cargo and I keep my word."

"Could we be refused landing rights on Temple Home?" Twilka voiced one of her primary concerns.

"No problem. I obtained special clearance from the Lady in White's temple," Nick said. "No one can override her approval, not even her sister."

CHAPTER SEVEN

As the *Space Dragon* arrived in orbit and Rafferty argued with planetary authorities about landing rights, Nick received a message from the Renegade, notifying them he'd be ready to discuss options as soon as the ship was gear down at the spaceport.

Sure enough, he came aboard within minutes of the landing and Casey escorted him to where Twilka and the others waited in the mess.

"Have you seen him? Is he all right?" She was pacing, unable to sit still, and whirled to confront Quaid as he crossed the threshold into the dining chamber.

"I have not seen him yet, but I have been assured he's fine. A little worse for wear, perhaps, which is to be expected. Harbin was zealous in his mission to capture Khevan and bring him home to the Lady." Quaid glanced around the mess. "Do you have any coffee made? My throat is dry from all the talking I've been doing since I got to Temple Home."

Casey set a mug of freshly brewed coffee on the table and retreated to the kitchen area.

After sliding into the empty chair in front of the mug, Quaid stretched his long legs, took a drink of the coffee, and murmured his satisfaction. Head tilted, eyes narrowed, he examined Twilka. "You may as well sit. This discussion will take time and you're hovering like a small bird of prey."

She yanked a chair out and plunked herself next to Mara. "I want to be in action, going to see him, getting him out of there, not sitting here drinking coffee."

"Patience," Quaid said. "I've had an audience with the Red Lady. She's extremely angry over Khevan's betrayal of his oath for a second time. He's been sentenced to death, of course, and she's devising the means, fueled by every drop of venom and hate in her being. He will be made to suffer for a protracted time and beg for death repeatedly before she's done. No human can withstand the full brunt of her fury."

"So there's no hope?" Twilka felt hot tears spill. *I haven't cried this much in my entire life. Got to get a grip here.* She swiped her cheeks.

"I didn't say anything remotely so dire." He held up one hand as his lips twitched in obvious amusement. "Patience isn't your strong suit, is it? I believe there's one possibility."

"Remote, judging by your tone." Nick reached over and clasped Mara's hand. "What do we need to do?"

"I spent considerable time in the library at the Temple of the Lady in White and consulted with her Senior Monk before I approached the goddess of flames." He held up a hand and stared at Twilka. "No, the Lady in White won't help. This is between her sister goddess and a man who swore an oath he now wants to break. Try to remember, no matter how much you love him, his sworn word is the crux of the matter."

Nodding, biting her lip, Twilka forced herself to say nothing.

He studied her for a moment, then relented as he addressed her in a softer voice. "I understand neither of you takes his oath breaking lightly. I understand you love each other. I'm impressed by the ferocity and depth of your connection. I envy the bond. But we need to remember the Red Lady is completely within her rights here."

Twilka wiped her cheeks. "So what do we do now?"

"I had a faint memory, which I confirmed with her sister's people, that opened the door to a single, dangerous possibility. Khevan is an extremely senior Brother. At his level, he has the right, under the Lady's own laws, to request a ceremony known as *merdamier* in her language—that's the closest a human can come to the pronunciation," he said as if in apology.

"You mentioned that to us before," Twilka said. "What exactly is involved?"

"I've refreshed my memory and confirmed a few details. *Merdamier* is a series of challenges, set for the Brother by the Lady, which he must overcome in the space of one night, from sunset to sunrise. If he fails at any of the challenges, he dies. It is a clean, quick death."

Twilka preferred to focus on possibilities. "And if he survives?"

"He goes free, his oath is sundered, and his connection to the Red Lady severed, which is what is desired in this case, of course."

"What kind of tests?" asked Mara.

"And where would we come into it?" Nick wanted to know. "Or do we?"

"The Red Lady is an alien being, immeasurably old, with control over space and time. She can set any challenge she desires," Quaid said. "Anything she thinks will cause the petitioner to fail. As far as we can tell, the petitioner is physically transported to whatever environment she creates for each test. Real, for all intents and purposes, but yet not occurring in the actual world as we know it."

"So she could plunge him into a solar flare or something?" Twilka said in horror. "How are these rules fair?"

"As far as we could tell from the old documents in the library, the tests must be rooted in the petitioner's experiences to a certain extent. So he has a measurable chance of winning through each one, no matter how slight. Although the final phase of the last challenge—if he survives to reach the closing moments of the night—will most likely be mortal combat, because the basis of her organization is physical life and death. The records are vague about the final resolution, probably because so few have ever survived. This ceremony has been invoked rarely, as you might expect. The White Lady's Senior Monk has volunteered to act as a neutral party, by the way, and monitor the proceedings."

"And us?" Nick asked again. "How can we help Khevan?"

"The petitioner is allowed, encouraged even, to have one to three comrades in arms who will stand with him and help him—or hinder him as the case may be—in the challenges." The Renegade stared at them over the lip of his coffee mug, one eyebrow raised, as if asking a question.

"I'll stand with him through the entire ordeal," Twilka said. "It's my right—my duty. It's our problem, not Nick and Mara's."

"I'd be the most likely to survive," Nick said. "I've been in mortal combat more than once. I'm not trying to insult you ladies, but going up against D'nvannae Brothers in hand-to-hand combat isn't for the untrained, no matter how valiant."

"Before we continue, I need to caution you that if the comrade dies in the challenge environment the Red Lady creates, the person perishes in real life as well." Quaid took a sandwich from a tray Casey brought to the table. "The risks are as high for you as they are for Khevan. The Lady will show no mercy."

"Doesn't matter. I'll take the chance," Nick said.

"I'm not afraid," Twilka spoke on top of his words.

"I'm in. I can handle myself." Mara was less outspoken, but pugnaciously determined.

"Raff and I can help." Casey leaned on the bulkhead. "We don't know Khevan as well as these guys do, but he's a stand up warrior and he'd do the same for us."

The Renegade shook his head. "Your willingness to stand with your friend does you all honor. As it happens, the Lady has set the stakes. She believes each of you three played a role in Khevan straying from her path, although, of course, she blames Twilka most of all. She'll allow only the three of you, one for each challenge—Mara first, Nick next, and Twilka last, which would be the stage with mortal combat. I believe the first challenge is the most survivable. She may even try to win him to her side once more."

"So she thinks I'm the least of us?" Mara said, stiffening her spine and frowning. "I'm not sure I like that."

Quaid remained unruffled. "I know she has the least animosity toward you. One should never try too hard to outthink the Red Lady."

"What does a D'nvannae Brother who participates on the side of the oath breaker get out of it? Wouldn't the Lady be angry with them?" Twilka asked.

"It can be a way to curry her favor. What if Harbin, for example, volunteered? Would you trust him to watch Khevan's back? His 'six' as our friend Nick would say?"

Mouth dropping open, she fell against the chair cushions for a second before she said, "Only to stab him."

"Exactly. Thus pleasing the Lady. Or, if a Brother was a true ally of Khevan's, he might win the Lady's respect through a valiant showing in the challenges. The point is moot because she can override his right to select his allies and she has chosen the three of you, in that order. You can, of course, refuse."

Khevan sat on the cot in the cold cell, wondering how much longer the Lady intended to keep him in suspense before she killed him. If she was waiting for him to change his mind, it would be a cold day in hell. *She'd have to administer more years of torture and now she understands nothing she can do to me will change my love for Twilka.* The goddess would surely decree such unforgivable rebellion needed a dramatic end. *Probably a public execution, as an example to anyone else thinking about straying. Or to intimidate anyone among my allies who didn't switch sides fast enough.* He was mildly curious whether she was going to consume him with her flames or have Harbin execute him in a staged battle after she'd tortured him enough to slake her anger and thirst for revenge.

At least I managed to save Twilka. Her life was out of his hands now, but the Red Lady kept her word, no matter what her other qualities might be. There'd be no further retribution against the human woman, not unless someone new took out a contract on her. With a small flicker of happiness that threatened to break his iron self-control he indulged in a moment of memory, savoring the thought of how soft and warm his beloved's skin felt to touch. *At least we had one chance to make things right between us. She knows how much she meant to me.*

He hadn't told her the entire truth—when he'd emerged from the hell the Red Lady put him through to reindoctrinate him, he'd come close to going rogue and killing the man he believed had taken his place in Twilka's life. Realizing his hands were clenched into fists as the fury of the memory rode him, he took a deep breath and rolled his shoulders. Only the belief in her happiness, the conviction she didn't think of him anymore, had enabled Khevan to master his jealous rage at the time. A portion of the emotion was undoubtedly spillover from the Red Lady's influence, but jealousy had burned a hole in his heart. Thinking Twilka cared for another man the way he wanted her to love him had been like a wound to his heart that never healed. But her happiness and safety were his paramount concerns, no matter what, so he'd made himself stay away from wherever she was reported to be. He kept up with any crumb of news he could glean about her.

And now I know the truth of her love for me. So much time lost, wasted, because of the Red Lady. I gave her my oath in good faith so many years ago—why can't she be gracious and release me after all I've done in her name? Is that so much for a loyal servant to ask? He straightened, pushing away the regrets that he and Twilka wouldn't have the opportunity to build a life together. As unlikely a couple as the two of them seemed on the surface, somehow they belonged to each other. He could go to his death with that certainty as comfort.

He worried about the way he'd had to leave her, injured and helpless in the alley after Harbin struck her. *I hope I get one final chance at the bastard, if the Lady decrees any kind of contest between us as part of my death.* He wished there was a way to know for sure Twilka was all right, safely rescued from the streets by Nick and Mara. Not knowing how she was recovering tore at him.

Creaking and groaning from the cumbersome, old fashioned wooden cell door startled him. He wasn't allowed visitors and this wasn't his one daily mealtime. The door swung open as two Brothers, bristling with weapons, stepped into the chamber, staring at Khevan as if daring him to try an attack. He stayed on the cot, hands behind his head, affecting unconcern, not wasting his breath on asking any questions. If it was time to meet his fate, he'd find out soon enough. This low ranking pair weren't here to kill him.

Harbin sauntered across the threshold, smiling, as always, at the sight of his imprisoned rival, barefoot, reduced to wearing the rough rags of a penitent. "You have a visitor," he said with a flourish.

"That will be all." The man who walked into the cell behind Harbin dismissed the high-ranking D'nvannae as if he was a gnat. "I'll knock when I've concluded my conversation with the prisoner. Leave us."

Instinctively, Khevan rose and stood at attention while Harbin and his men retreated, closing the door. The visitor was a confusing apparition with the arrogant demeanor of a supreme Brother, clad in the fine black leather, yet he had no facial tattoo.

"Be at ease. Please, sit." The man knocked on the door and it opened immediately. "I require a chair, fool."

"At once, sir." In less than a minute, the guard brought in a seat and placed it close to the door. He saluted and left.

Khevan watched this with bemusement.

Extending his hand, the guest said, "I'm Quaid Jacq, and I'm going to be your advocate during the ceremony of *merdamier*."

Shaking hands automatically, Khevan said, "I haven't requested the trial. The Lady made it clear I'd die in the flames or in a staged ritual combat. As far as I know, she's still making up her mind which will be more painful."

"Yes, well, fortunately for you, I reminded her of her own law. A man at your rank has the right to the ritual, the chance to leave the Brotherhood free and clear since he can no longer serve her in good faith. And a clean, fast death if he fails." Quaid's eyes narrowed. "I have it on excellent authority your freedom is what you desire. Are my informants wrong?"

A vision of Twilka flashed before Khevan's eyes. To be free of his oath, to go to her would be astonishing, more than he dared dream of. Ruthlessly, he quashed the wild hope. "No one will stand with me. Those who were my allies are either dead or too afraid. I'd refuse anyone she chose. Are you proposing to take part on my side?"

Quaid shook his head, the gleaming blond hair caught in a ponytail. "Alas, much as I relish a new challenge and a good fight, no. By the terms of my pre-existing agreement with the Lady, I can't."

Khevan had it worked out now. "You're the Renegade? I thought you were nothing but a legend."

Quaid punched him lightly in the shoulder. "Quite real. My help has been sought by those who care about you, outside these walls. Impressive allies."

"No." Horrified at the mere idea, Khevan rose, pacing in the small cell. "They mustn't risk themselves; *she* mustn't set foot on this planet." He was reluctant to utter Twilka's name inside these walls. "My friends don't know—they can't possibly navigate *merdamier*—what false hope did you give them?"

Quaid didn't show any sign of taking offense at the rejection of his efforts. "My understanding was you and these allies had stood together through another test of life and death, and won your freedom. With them at your side…"

"No. They mustn't come here. Tell them I'm grateful but they need to stay away from Temple Home."

"Your friends are already here, having landed this morning. The ritual will be tomorrow night, from dusk till dawn," Quaid said.

"I'll refuse to participate. I'll demand the Lady kill me or have me killed." Khevan's frustration and fear for Twilka were practically choking him. He had to find the right words to make this uninvited meddler understand. "Everything I did for the last five years was in support of my love for Twilka, to keep her alive. Safe. If she puts herself into the Red Lady's hands now…" He shook his head as Quaid sat, unmoved. "I'll be dying for nothing and so will Twilka."

"Or you might both be alive and free at the end of the night." Quaid rose. "It is, of course, your choice, but be aware your friends and the woman you love will be there, will watch you die if you give up without a fight. Knowing our charming Lady of the Flames as I do, she'll take great pleasure in prolonging your death to torment Twilka in particular. Do you want her to have those as her final memories of you?"

Khevan was silent for a moment, searching for loopholes and finding none. "The Lady's already granted their request to stand with me?"

"I think the idea amuses her. Novelty is enticing to a millennia-old goddess and she couldn't resist this twist. I counted on her reaction, in fact." Quaid went to the door, disdaining the chair. Clearly, it wasn't his job to remove it from the cell. "I'll rejoin you at dinnertime tomorrow, make sure you're given the proper meal and all the weapons and clothing your rank demands. I'll stand at your shoulder as you enter the ceremonial space." He rapped on the panel and glanced over his shoulder at Khevan. "Think long and hard about throwing away the sacrifice your friends and your woman are prepared to make."

The door opened and the Renegade was gone. A guard edged into the cell and snatched the chair, lest Khevan have one thing more than he was supposed to and derive comfort from the fact. The door slammed and he heard the lock close. At least he was to be spared any more of Harbin's taunting.

He reclined on the lumpy, straw filled mattress, hands behind his head, and tried to order his thoughts, to decide what to do. No one knew exactly what *merdamier* involved, doubtless arduous mental and physical tests the Red Lady would devise, based on the person being examined, but all members of the Brotherhood were aware it had been hundreds of years, if ever, since anyone at his level had won freedom from their vows. The idea hadn't even crossed his mind, if truth be told.

Nick, Mara, and most of all Twilka were staunch allies, but how could they hope to defeat the Lady's worst efforts? But if the three of them were determined to stand with him, he had to give his supreme effort to the challenge.

Chapter Eight

True to his word, the Renegade reappeared with the evening meal the next night, helping himself to a few of the choicer morsels as Khevan cast aside the rough penitent's robe, bathed in the tub the temple's servants filled with hot water, dressed in his black leather uniform, and strapped his knives on. "I made sure your own blades were returned to you," Quaid said, sipping his wine. "Apparently, someone had taken it upon himself to confiscate them prematurely."

Khevan paused as he fastened his shirt. "Harbin?"

"He overestimates his rank at the moment, which will bring him to grief if he's not careful." With a wicked grin, the Renegade took a slice of cheese. "I was also clear with the kitchen I'd be sharing your meal, and if there was any attempt to poison or drug you, I'd be the first to suffer. Which the Lady would *not* regard with favor. You have many enemies in the order, which goes to show how well regarded you were by the Lady." He sounded admiring.

"A distinction I could have done without." Khevan sat at the table which had been brought in and served himself a steak.

"Your friends and your woman are here, and I've tried to explain how this ceremony may work," Quaid said, while Khevan choked down fine Azrigone beef, knowing he needed energy for the ordeal ahead. "The Lady in White's soldiers will escort them into and out of the chamber, to ensure there are no...accidents. Her Chief Monk has agreed to judge the contest. Our goddess accepts his jurisdiction, which did rather surprise me. I wonder if the sisters have discussed this, unbeknownst to us mere mortals." He took another morsel of the cheese.

"I'm grateful for your help with the arrangements." Khevan wasn't in the mood for conversation. He needed to settle his mind, and be at his sharpest for whatever the Red Lady might throw at him. Twilka's life depended on it.

"A number of your Brothers—and one of the Sisterhood—have come to me secretly in the last day, offering to stand with you in place of the outsiders." Quaid studied the fruit on the side plate and plucked a handful of golden berries. "I think some of them actually have loyalty to you, or believe you might have a chance, and therefore their standing would be immeasurably enhanced if they stood by your side. Hard to know the true motives, the Brotherhood is so rife with plots and games. And the Sisters have their own intricate maneuvers of power, which no mere human such as you or I can hope to comprehend."

"I want no one but Nick, Mara, and Twilka," Khevan said. "Since the prize on the line is my life, and freedom to leave the order, those three are the only ones I trust to have at my back." He shot the Renegade a look. "Present company excepted, of course."

"Understood. I rejected all the offers on your behalf. The Lady made her will clear to me in any case—only the three outsiders would be allowed to participate."

"Thank you."

"At least a few in the order's ranks were kindly disposed to your quest."

"The only one who matters is the Red Lady, and she's livid I chose Twilka over her."

Khevan and Quaid walked through the corridors in the dank dungeon area under the temple, escorted by Harbin and ten Brothers with drawn blasters. He found their fear of him amusing. As if he'd try to escape now, at the last moment.

In the upper hallway, the Senior Monk from the Lady in White's temple waited, leaning on his gnarled staff, the translucent crystal at the top glowing faintly. Straightening with an audible crack of his spine, the monk eyed Khevan for a moment.

"Is it still your intention to undergo the challenges of *merdamier,* no matter what the Red Lady may present to you?"

Khevan stood at attention, gazing at a point above the elderly monk's head. "It is, sir."

"You understand your life and the lives of your allies may be immediately forfeit if any challenge is failed? And you swear to abide by my rulings?"

Now he lowered his eyes to meet the man's assessing stare. "I do."

"It is well. The chamber for the challenge awaits." The monk pointed his staff in the direction he wished them to proceed.

Khevan wondered where his friends were and if he'd have any chance to speak to them before the night of trials commenced. He marched next to the Renegade, disoriented, feeling as if he was standing to the side, out of body. If Quaid hadn't thought to safeguard his dinner by sharing it, he'd suspect he was drugged. The idea he was going to undergo *merdamier,* with Twilka and the others involved, was unfathomable.

He entered an area of the temple he'd never seen before or set foot in. The elderly monk proceeded, surefooted, as if he knew exactly where he was going in the twisting hallways. Khevan speculated how old the man was. Could he have been alive for the last *merdamier,* centuries ago? There were rumors the goddesses could grant near immortal life to their favored adherents. He gave himself a mental shake, trying to gather his wandering wits. The Red Lady was liable to throw anything and everything at him during this night and he needed to focus.

Two senior D'nvannae Brothers were standing guard at a pair of tall wooden doors, embossed with symbols in the Lady's language, accented lavishly in gold leaf. As the group approached, the men opened the portals, and Khevan stepped across the threshold. It was a large chamber, with an ornate throne on an elevated platform at the front, sitting on a dais worked with tariqnas, their wings, necks, and tails entwined in an erotic dance.

The doors closed behind him with a thump and he realized he'd come to a halt, mesmerized by the Lady's throne.

The monk indicated Khevan and the Renegade were to step into an enclosure guarded by a waist-high rail, dark wood, gleaming with polish, supported at regular intervals by more tariqnas, carved from various types of wood. A simple wooden bench sat in the exact center of the space.

"You will take your place here and remain standing until the Lady has entered and seated herself." The monk closed the gate behind them and moved to stand on a raised dais to the left. There was a throne there as well, although the monk chose not to sit. This throne was carved from a mixture of gleaming white substances, like bone or opal, with the outline of nebulae on the back and sides, accented by sparkling gemstones. The central nebula on the throne had a significant resemblance to a tariqna in shape. Khevan wondered if the fabled home planet of the sisters lay in the depicted star formation. A smaller, wooden chair had been placed incongruously to the side for the occasion.

"Where are the others?" Khevan whispered to Quaid.

Before his companion could answer, the doors opened with a whoosh and three monks of the White Brotherhood paced into the room, each paired with one of Khevan's friends. Nick and Mara were hand in hand, faces set in serious expressions. Nick sketched a casual salute and Mara gave him a small wave. Twilka came last in the line, searching the room for him. Her lush lips curved upward with happiness and she sighed with obvious relief when her eyes met Khevan's.

He shook his head, although he allowed himself a small smile for her. Best not to say anything. His adrenaline was spiking, worried for her safety, for the safety of all three of them, and he had to avert his gaze, take a deep breath, and run through a meditation chain to center his emotions for combat. The longing to go to Twilka and hold her in his arms was hard to resist, but he had to call on all his self-discipline to endure the night ahead. He couldn't breach the protocol and risk unknown consequences for both of them. On the surface, she appeared to be recovered, no bruises from the blow Harbin had given her in the street.

His three allies took their place in another enclosure to the right, with a monk standing behind each.

A gong sounded and there was a blast of heat and light as black and purple flames exploded into life, encircling the red throne at the front of the chamber, drawing all eyes. A moment later, the Red Lady of D'nvannae sat there, at ease, smiling, beautiful in a form fitting scarlet dress. She'd manifested in a lush representation calculated to appeal to human males.

The Senior Monk bowed to her. "We are all assembled, my Lady, and ready to begin the challenges at your pleasure. The sun sets at this moment."

She nodded and transferred her attention to Khevan, glaring at him with her brow furrowed. "Any last words, oath breaker?"

"No, my Lady." There was nothing he could say or do now.

Lips tight, the Lady flicked her left hand and a section of the floor in front of her throne disappeared, replaced by a circular pit, lined in flat sheets of ruby, with deep channels of obsidian and jet running between the gems. The depression was ten feet in diameter and the air above it shimmered, as if heated by a desert sun.

"Explain this to the participants," she said to the monk, "Since not all are of my Order."

"The Lady chooses the time, the setting, and the nature of the challenges, and creates the reality into which the oath breaker and his ally will be physically placed." Gesturing at the oval, he added, "We here in the chamber will be able to watch the events transpire, in order for me to reach judgments as to outcome."

In the next breath, he swung the butt of his staff to strike the large gong that had appeared from thin air. The sonorous note echoed in Khevan's head, filling his senses with sound, the vibrations driving him to his knees and blocking out his vision.

Dimly, he heard Mara gasp and Nick swearing.

Merdamier was underway.

He waited in the outer chamber, standing where the senior Brother in charge of pledges had told him to wait. Each boy came here alone, to reflect for a few moments on the choice he was making, to ready his mind for acceptance of the Red Lady's blessing, and to dedicate his life to her. Soon he'd see the Red Lady personally, as she accepted his oath and bound him to her service. It was said a few specially talented or lucky boys in each class received a visitation from the Lady in White while waiting here and were offered the choice to serve Her instead. He flicked his gaze sideways for a moment at a closed door set into the far wall. Rumor said if a boy chose to serve the Lady in White, he exited through that door, which would open only to him for a few moments. He'd be banned from the Red Lady's temple for life. Khevan admitted to a bit of sneaking curiosity what it'd be like to glimpse the Lady his mother had so admired, but he didn't want the distraction.

Maybe less determined boys need time to gather their courage, but I don't need any time for reflection. No second thoughts or regrets for me.

Despite his defiant attitude, Khevan shivered a bit and shifted on the stone, cold beneath his bare feet. He tried to stoke his courage with the fire of his anger against his stepfather, but the emotions wouldn't come, overridden by the knowledge he was about to face one of the most feared and unpredictable sentients in the Sectors. *What if she rejects me?* He'd worked hard in the training classes and was counted at the top of his age level, but the instructors emphasized over and over the warning one shouldn't assume anything where the Red Lady was concerned. *She has to accept me—I'll swear to whatever she wants.*

Waiting was eating at him. The room was cold; his supplicant robe a thin and scant barrier against the chill. Was this part of her testing of the applicants?

Footsteps sounded in the corridor behind him and he pivoted, alarmed. The D'nvannae in charge had told him he'd be left in solitude until it was his moment to see their Lady. Was someone coming to remove him before he had his chance to bond with her? Had he already failed without recognizing a test?

An ordinary human woman stepped into the room. Blonde and beautiful, she was dressed in a black tunic worn over blue leggings, her shoes expensive embossed leather, and her only jewelry an old-fashioned gold wedding ring on her left hand. "Khevan?"

Although he wanted to sag with relief, he went on the offensive instead, as he'd been taught, assuming a combat-ready stance. "How do you know my name? Who are you?"

"I'm Mara." Head tilted, she waited, as if expecting him to recognize her. "You don't know me at all, do you?"

Seeing no threat in her, he relied on the fledgling social skills the monks had been drumming into him and the other recruits from the lower rungs of galactic society. Stepping back from the aggressive pose he'd assumed, he bowed. "No, my lady, I'm sorry, I don't."

"It's all right; I hardly recognize you, although the truth is we didn't meet until you were a grown man. But we are friends. Or will be." She looked around the chamber, touching the nearest tapestry. "Where are we?"

"In the antechamber to the Oath Room." How could she be unaware of her location? "I'm the next applicant to give my life to the Red Lady."

Mara walked to the bench. "May I?" Without waiting for permission, she sat and patted the cushioned surface beside her in invitation.

Still confused by her presence, he sat at the other end. She wore a spicy perfume, reminding him of someone or something lost to him. A twinge of intense sorrow pierced his thoughts and his heart. He shook the effect off with an impatient snort.

"Why are you choosing to serve the Red Lady?" she asked.

"A foolish question. I plan to become the most highly trained and honored D'nvannae Brother ever to serve her," he said, sitting straight-backed and proud.

"Why? Is it the power? The fame? Do you believe all her promises?"

Confiding the real reason was tempting. This woman seemed important to him personally, a friend as she herself had said, although he'd no idea who she was. Astonishing himself, he decided to trust her. Leaning closer, he said in a low voice meant to carry only to her ears, "I join so I can kill my stepfather."

This Mara was made of stern stuff, not flinching from the hatred he injected into his declaration, although her blue eyes widened. Biting her lip, she asked, "Did he kill your mother?"

Khevan lowered his eyes, as scenes of his mother's sad death flooded his mind. "Yes."

Voice soft, Mara asked her next question. "Do you think she'd want you to sign up for a lifetime of killing and blood? Would she want you to honor her memory in such a way?"

"I-I can't remember her," he said, furious with himself over the tears burning in his eyes. "Except for how she died."

Mara closed the gap between them and gave him a hug. "I'm sure she loved you very much."

"Then why did she stay with him? He beat both of us and then he finally went too far. Those memories are seared into my brain. I thought I was big enough now to stop him, but I failed, and he killed her, threw her down the stairs and broke her neck, staged the scene to support his lies of her death being an accident. No one would believe me about what really happened. The police didn't care if I was a witness, or whether I too bore the bruises of his anger. The Brothers will make sure I'm strong enough, deadly enough to kill him when I seek him out. I'll have my revenge. He sold me to their recruiter for a handful of credits, but the joke's on him—I *want* to be here." Hands clenched into fists, he shook with the anger rising through his body.

"Didn't your mother encourage you to serve the Lady in White? To be a warrior for good?"

How can this woman know these things about me, when I don't know her at all? His head was spinning. Suddenly, he had a vision of himself, sitting next to his mother on a rickety couch, heard her sweet, soft voice, telling him a story about a warrior of ancient times, riding a big black quadruped, carrying a sword and a shield, and rescuing weaker people from their enemies. "How do you know what my mother wanted? Were you her friend?"

"I never met her. You confide in me, a bit, during a difficult experience we'll have when you're a grown man." Leaning against the wall, Mara rubbed her forehead. "Nothing is simple."

"Your words are strange, talking as if you come from the future."

"In a way I have, I guess." She straightened her spine and took a deep breath, as if she had a task to accomplish. "What if you were to see both Ladies? If you had a choice today?" Mara asked, resting one hand on top of his fist.

Khevan swallowed hard. "I vowed to avenge my mother's death. I have to become a D'nvannae to carry out the execution. I'd choose Red."

The room filled with a bright white light, so stark he had to close his eyes against it.

"Such determination and dedication," said a new voice, lovely, yet with a sad inflection. "He refused then and refuses now to believe in other possibilities. He could have been one of my strongest, yet walked the other path from this moment forward. You cannot dissuade him, Mara."

"I know his choice was made long ago," the woman said, keeping her arm around him as if to protect him. "But I had to try."

He wanted to see the White Lady, for he knew the newcomer must be the goddess. He'd never have another chance. Opening his eyes, struggling to make out the form in the brilliant halo of white light, he rose and took a step away from Mara, slipping from her loose embrace. There was a slender figure behind the majestic White Lady. Unable to believe what he was seeing, Khevan blinked hard against the light. "Mother?"

"Khevan Adaranovic, the Lady of D'nvannae will take your oath now," said a sonorous male voice from the hallway. "Walk forward and pledge your life to her. The Red Lady waits."

He hesitated.

Mara left the bench and moved to stand with the Lady in White and the ghost of his mother.

"If I choose your service, will my mother return to me?" he asked.

"She's gone beyond this world, as you well know," the benevolent goddess said. "I bring her spirit to you this one time, so no matter what befalls you, you may have her memory as comfort. She was a true adherent of my teachings and beliefs. That you reject me and go to my sister's dark promises cannot be counted as a failing on *her* part."

The light reached out, touching his forehead with a sensation as if a feather had been drawn across his skin. A cascade of images and sensory memories flooded his mind. Instinctively, he created a mental block like a stone barricade to protect them, the way his mother had taught him when he as a young boy, so he'd always have these precious moments as comfort. The glowing shadow he believed was his mother floated across the floor to him, touching what might have been her hand to his heart for the space of a single breath, and then was gone.

"Twice in the whorls of time you've refused my service, my gifts," the Lady in White said. "Yet I wish you well, for all the potential to do good I see in your heart. I'll not return to you again, Khevan, but I left one door open the slightest crack." There was amusement in her voice as she said, "Things do come in threes, as you humans say. Yet this third possibility doesn't lie in your hands, for I won't be refused again. It will be the choice of another whether you're worthy of the gift." The Lady inclined her head to him and faded from view.

Only Mara was left.

"Khevan Adaranovic, the Red Lady waits." The voice echoed in the chamber, a hint of impatience in the clipped syllables.

In three quick steps, Mara was at his side and gave him a hug. He returned the embrace, saying in a whisper, "I don't know who you are, but thank you for trying to talk me out of my choice, for bringing the Lady of Light and my mother to me. I must go. If the herald calls a third time and I don't answer, my chance is lost."

"I don't know how real any of this is," Mara answered, smoothing his hair from his brow and framing his face with her hands for a moment before kissing him lightly on the forehead. "But I hope I helped."

"You did. Someday I'll repay you." Hand over his heart, he made the pledge sincerely, even as he stepped away from her.

"You already have."

Khevan spun on his heel, squared his shoulders, and paced into the corridor leading to the waiting Red Lady.

CHAPTER NINE

"The first challenge is a draw."

Khevan shook his head, disoriented, as the Head Monk of the White Lady's temple made his declaration. He gripped the railing in front of him tightly, to steady himself, and turned his head to search for Mara. Only Nick and Twilka stood in the designated square, their assigned monks behind the bench. He had a moment of panic such as he'd not experienced in years.

"Mara's fine," Quaid whispered quickly. "Her part in this is done and she's been allowed to leave. The Lady of Light's monk escorted her out while you were yet regaining consciousness."

Shooting another quick glance at Nick, reassured by his friend's calm demeanor, Khevan tried to focus on the Red Lady. *If Mara had come to any harm, Nick would be tearing this place apart.*

"He still chose my flames over my sister's light," said the Lady of the D'nvannae, raising her voice. "How is this counted as a draw?"

"In the process, he regained precious memories you'd extracted from him—of his mother and of the moment he met *my* lady, your sister." The aged monk was adamant, leaning on his staff, not the least bit cowed by the towering flames blazing orange, red, and black around the Red Lady's throne. "With the help of his friend, he overcame your power. Yet, undeniably, he did choose your service in the end, hence a draw."

"He remains mine." Her voice was greedy, possessive. "A D'nvannae subject to my will."

The monk inclined his head. "For the moment. Two trials remain."

"Prepare yourself—she'll make the next challenge harder," Quaid said.

Khevan opened his mouth to acknowledge the soft spoken warning and found himself alone, standing in the corridor of a spaceship. Pivoting slowly, hearing a recorded voice give warnings in the five official languages of the Sectors, he realized he was on the *Nebula Dream*. Piles of luggage, dropped items, here and there splashes of blood on the carpet or bulkhead testified to the terror and violence driving terrified passengers to seek escape from certain doom.

I need to find a lifeboat and get off this wreck myself.

A blinking green light at the curve of the corridor caught his eye. One lifeboat remaining, waiting for him. Of course the Lady would take care of him, make sure such a senior brother escaped the disaster. Smiling, he strode confidently to the portal, which was open, the short passageway that would take him to safety in the LB inviting. He raised his foot to step across the threshold and paused, gripping the edge of the portal with one hand.

This isn't right. This isn't what happened to me.

Confused, he shook his head, blinking. He heard voices faintly—a man shouting orders and a woman pleading for help to free people who were trapped. Nick? Mara? The names set off echoes in his mind, but when he checked in both directions, the main corridor was empty.

You have to go now. A voice in his head, the Lady's voice, insistent, annoyed. *Why do you hesitate?*

The lights blinked off, emergency lamps coming on again only in spots, the rest of the corridor nothing but pools of inky darkness. The deck shuddered under his feet and he heard a muted explosion. Indeed, there was no time, the ship was clearly dying and he didn't want to die with it. He had many years of service yet to give his Lady, with rewards to reap, and it was not part of her plan or his for him to perish ingloriously here. Turning, he took one step into the passage and the portal began to slide shut behind him.

Call upon me, if ever you or Mara are in need of help. I will come.

His own voice rang in his ears, making an unbreakable promise to a man who was like a brother of flesh and blood to him, not merely a fellow devotee of the Red Lady.

Khevan shoved his body into the diminishing gap, stopping the portal from closing. He checked the corridor again, but it remained darkened, empty as far as he could tell. He took a deep breath, noting the air was going bad, the oxygen depleted.

I'll come if you need me, my word as an officer, the other man, this brother, had sworn.

Nick *had* come to help him, and now Khevan was going to flee, breaking his own oath?

Without hesitation, Khevan forced himself past the pressure of the door and ran along the corridor toward the gravlift. *Nick and Mara must have gone ahead without me.* But he knew exactly where the couple would be and what peril they faced. Nick wouldn't survive without his help and there was precious little time. He flung himself into the crew gravlift, which functioned smoothly, carrying him upward to the deck he sought, even as the ship shuddered. He stumbled going into the Level Two corridor, which was again empty, but part of his mind whispered the absence of others was correct. No one had been here, except those they came to rescue.

The air rushed past, buffeting him, throwing debris at him. *Hull breach!* But no, this was wrong, not how it happened, not *when* it happened. Clenching his jaw, Khevan let go of his memory. He had to deal with the situation at hand and not be distracted by uncertain flickers of memory. "Nick?" he called repeatedly, checking the cabins as he strode past them, which took too much time, but if this wasn't the way he remembered the events, he couldn't take a chance on missing his friend.

Another lifeboat portal beckoned him, the green light warm and inviting in the gloom and terror of the corridor ravaged by turbulent wind, accompanied by the sounds of a hull breaking apart. Khevan ignored it, pulling himself onward, fighting the pull of the escaping atmosphere, which tried to hurl him back the way he'd come. He could almost believe the swirling wind was trying to toss him into the LB passageway.

Ahead, a twisted mass of wreckage blocked his path, a maze of broken bulkheads and dangerously buckled structural members, with AI ganglions and power conduits wreathing the mess like pit vipers. Nick must be on the other side. Holding onto a support beam to stabilize himself, eyes narrowed against the flying debris, Khevan studied the obstacle, searching for the best way in. "Nick?"

A hoarse shout answered his call. "Here! Don't risk yourself, pal; I'm trapped. Get out while there's time."

He would urge Khevan to save himself. Nick was a man of honor and self-sacrifice.

Khevan identified a potential path into the edge of the debris and edged forward. "Hold on; I'm coming. We'll escape together."

He was making progress, ducking and weaving and crawling on the deck at one point, when suddenly flames broke out directly ahead of him. Rising to his feet in a clear space, Khevan understood the fire was no natural phenomenon, but the unmistakable sign of the Lady's presence, all oranges and reds laced with black. Her face formed inside the flames, eyes gleaming eerily scarlet.

"I order you to retreat, cease this useless effort. There is no contract with this man, you owe him nothing and you owe me everything."

"I refuse to leave him. If the situation was reversed, Nick wouldn't abandon me. His kind of warrior never leaves anyone behind. I can do no less." He forged ahead, the flames retreating as he pushed his way through the next complicated tangle. A dangling wire shocked him, fat sparks flying in the wind. He realized his leather jacket had been burned through, revealing scorched and blackened skin beneath. Pushing away the pain, Khevan moved left, shifting a piece of wall and gaining a few yards. Tantalizing clear space lay ahead. "I'm nearly through," he shouted, trying to encourage his friend, hoping the words could be heard over the gale force wind.

Moving like snakes, AI ganglions wrapped themselves around his legs, rendering him immobile. He fell heavily into the debris, nearly impaling himself on a protruding metal spike. Another gashed his forehead and blood dripped into his eyes. As the ganglions tried to cocoon him, he managed to draw his D'nvannae dagger and slash at them with his good arm. Crawling as best he could, wielding the knife, he made it to the edge of the obstruction and rolled free.

Nick lay half in, half out of a cabin door, tons of debris pinning his legs. Khevan knew the impossibility of freeing the soldier in time.

"Told you to retreat," Nick said with an effort at a grin, although his face was taut with pain. "Your Lady changed things up on us like the bitch she is. Caught me here the moment the challenge began. I thought I heard the kids, worked my way inside, but the cabin was empty."

"Doubtless a trick on her part."

"Yeah, I figured. And then she collapsed the whole place around me as I was trying to escape, to go find you." Nick coughed up blood as acrid smoke wafted across the deck. "Didn't realize I was only here to act as bait to pull you off your objective."

Despite the dire circumstances, Khevan laughed as yet another lifeboat portal materialized on his left, soft lights glowing in invitation. The Red Lady wasn't being subtle at all. "There weren't *enough* lifeboats on the *Dream*," he shouted. "Stop throwing them at me—I won't be tempted."

He dragged himself to the cabin door, next to where Nick sprawled. Examining the debris pinning his friend, Khevan sought to shift the largest pieces. "If I can free you, we can get to one of the lifeboats the Lady keeps offering me." He put all his strength into tugging at a shard of corridor wall, ignoring the searing pain from his burned arm.

Nick shouted a curse. "Fuck, that hurts. Khevan, stop. I can't feel my legs anymore, but whatever you're doing feels like I'm being cut in half."

Khevan released the fragment of wood and metal and sank to his knees next to Nick as the entire ship shuddered around him.

"Guess we're not gonna make it this time," Nick said, fighting to get the words out, blood oozing from the corner of his mouth.

"Then we'll die together."

"Sorry I wasn't more help." Nick extended his right hand and they gripped each other's forearms tightly, two comrades who'd fought a good battle side by side.

"Your presence clarified many things for me, made my decisions good ones. I couldn't have asked for a better ally."

The lights flickered and went out as the sound of rending metal and escaping atmosphere became a terrible cacophony. Khevan couldn't hear himself think. He closed his eyes and held onto Nick as the one anchor he could trust in a mad world as the breath was sucked from his chest and he knew he was about to pass out.

"The Brother has won the second challenge. He followed his own path, refusing your orders and your enticements." The elderly priest pointed his staff at the goddess. "Although you made it impossible for him to rescue his friend, he remained unswerving in his determination."

Although the flames pulsed and roared around the throne, there was no argument from the Red Lady. She sat semi reclined, examining her elaborately decorated fingernails and not sparing so much as a glance for either the monk or Khevan.

Disoriented by the sudden end to the trip to the re-creation of the dying *Nebula Dream*, Khevan checked his arm, finding the jacket's sleeve intact. Flexing his muscles and making a fist brought no sensation of pain. He shot a glance at the enclosure where his allies had been and found only Twilka, who raised her hand in a small wave. Grabbing the Renegade's shoulder, he choked out his friend's name in the form of a question. "Nick?"

"Since you won the challenge, he survived and is whole." Quaid shook his head. "The Lady is determined to defeat you. The last round was perilously close. If Nick had died before you reached him, I'm not sure the victory would have gone to you, despite your efforts to save him. Your friend would have perished here, in real life also. I hope you and your woman can come through the final round."

"Any tips?"

"You're in unprecedented territory, my friend." Quaid swung around to stare at Twilka. "Do you believe she's up to taking on whatever the Red Lady throws at her? Could she survive a scenario like the one Nick just endured?"

"I never wanted her to be in any danger at all," he said, "But not because I doubted her heart or her strength. She'd do whatever is required."

"She's a Socialite, yes?"

"Among other things she's done and experienced." Annoyance at the implied criticism of Twilka made his voice curt. "There's much more to her."

"I was impressed with her determination to rescue you when I first met her, but whether that will be enough…"

Khevan turned to look at Twilka, who blew him an airy kiss, as if unconcerned by what lay ahead. He wasn't deceived, noting the lines of strain bracketing her eyes and lips. She seemed ten years older today and he regretted bringing her to this state. "We'll meet whatever is thrown at us together."

Twilka cowered, back to the wall, surrounded by men in a ring three deep. The would-be assailants were literally faceless, as in her worst nightmares, only blank skin where eyes and other features should be. Hands curved into claws reached to grab at her and she slapped them away, cursing and kicking. She sidled to the right and her opponents moved in lockstep with her. Nearly tripping over an empty vodka bottle, which rolled away on the deck, she realized she was wearing the navy blue-and-gold silk dress she'd worn on the night the *Nebula Dream* wrecked. "I hate this fucking dress," she screamed, shaking her fist at the ceiling. "I burned it. This isn't real; you're not real," she yelled at the eerily silent male figures, so angry she was spitting. "It's a fever dream from the Red Bitch. When Khevan gets here, you'll all be sorry. I'd run now, if I were you." Quickly, she ducked to grab another bottle from the deck, swinging it at a man who came too close, smashing it across his smooth face in a spray of broken glass and brandy. He reeled away, falling in a silent heap on the deck, bleeding heavily, and another took his place.

Uncannily mute, the circle closed in on her. The original mob had been cursing at her, making lewd remarks about their plans for her. The current silence helped her center on the fact that this wasn't real; she hadn't been catapulted through time into the actual horror of the *Nebula Dream*. She felt an oasis of calm at her core. *I've got this; I know what to do.* Having just watched Khevan and Nick struggle on a different version of the *Nebula Dream* gave her a starting point, an anchor for her efforts to stay focused. The Red Lady had tipped her hand just a bit.

A huge, ornamental vase full of faux branches blocked her path. The men pulled at her, hard, their hold on her arms and legs firm and unbreakable. Kicking and cursing, she was dragged into the center of the hall and lifted into the air on her back, as if in an obscene dance or as a sacrifice.

"Khevan!" Twilka screamed so hard her throat was raw. *Where in the seven hells was he? This was supposed to be a battle we'd fight together, wasn't it? So why am I alone in a version of my worst nightmare?*

A flicker of black in her peripheral vision caught her attention and she craned her neck, relief flooding over her. He'd come.

"In need of D'nvannae assistance?" A cold, sick feeling flooded through her body as she realized the newcomer was Harbin, leaning against the bulkhead, arms crossed, with a nonchalant smirk on his face. "Can you pay? What will you trade me to help you? No use waiting for Khevan. He doesn't care enough about you to risk himself here on this ship again."

The men or creatures holding her went motionless, as if his voice was a signal, and Twilka squirmed until she was free of their grasp, falling to the deck with bone bruising force. Rubbing her sore tailbone with one hand, she pointed the other at Harbin. "You're a liar. The Red Lady must be preventing him from coming to save me or he'd be here. You're the last person I'd ever ask for help." She scrabbled a few feet away and then rose to her feet, breaking into a run in the direction of the casino, where colorful lights blinked. She felt like she was wading through thick mud, unable to accelerate enough to escape. Terrified again, she glanced over her shoulder to find Harbin strolling slowly after her. The faceless men had disappeared.

Red Lady's mind tricks. She tried to run faster, although her knee and her tailbone ached from the fall.

"You have to find him or both your lives are forfeit," Harbin called out helpfully. "Although, if you do locate him, then of course I'll be called upon to kill you both."

The lights were on in the casino and she could hear the clinking and chiming from games of chance apparently running on automatic, but no people anywhere. Who could help her anyway? Only Khevan. Everyone else she might encounter would be a servant of the Red Lady. Tense because time was growing short, she hobbled past the entrance and realized she'd reached the crew gravlift. Choking back a sob, she leaned against the wall and opened the door with the code Mara had taught her so long ago, in the real *Nebula Dream*. Her hands were shaking so badly it took her two tries. The portal slid open with a click and she leaned over, dizzy and nauseous at the sight of the tube going straight to the bottom of the ship. Closing her eyes, afraid of fainting, she collapsed against the bulkhead, barely remaining on her feet. *There's no time to indulge in a panic attack over the height. Khevan's trapped somewhere in the Red Lady's web and he needs me.* Drawing a deep breath against the tightness in her chest, she stepped into the void, praying to the Lords of Space that the vengeful goddess had provided antigrav in her version of the *Dream*. The mechanism caught her as it was supposed to and gently let her drift down the levels of the ship.

She heard the sound of clapping above her. Craning her neck, she stared at Harbin, peering over the edge. Raising his voice, he called to her, "Well done. I didn't think you had it in you. But, never fear, we'll meet again before this is over."

Where in the seven hells am I supposed to be going? Why isn't Khevan with me and where can he be? Twilka racked her brain, searched her memories, and decided to try the cargo hold, based on their real experiences on the actual *Nebula Dream*. The Red Lady seemed to be applying twisted logic to her choices of scenario. Emerging from the gravlift, Twilka skidded to a halt. Instead of standing on a utilitarian deck, crammed with containers and equipment, she was on a dais in the center of a glossy black floor, where actual stars glittered, like the night sky. It was as if she'd been deposited in the middle of a galaxy. The gravlift and all vestiges of the faux *Nebula Dream* vanished like the illusions they were. Surrounding her were shelves, tables, pedestals, antigrav brackets, and cases full of objects—ornamental boxes, statues, paintings, clocks, elaborate stained glass, holograms, crystals, jewelry, books, scrolls, items she had no name for. The treasures were arranged apparently at random, lacking any organizational scheme she could detect.

"Do you like my collection?"

Twilka startled as the Red Lady herself strolled into view, barefoot, wearing a diaphanous, body hugging red gown, flames like a sun's corona framing the piquant heart-shaped face she'd chosen to display since the start of *merdamier*. "These represent every Brother who ever perished in my service. I promise them a place in my memories and I keep my word, for I am infinite in my capabilities." She picked up a small enameled figurine of a bird with two heads and examined the details for a moment before replacing it with utmost care. "I link each man's identity to an item which pleases me to gaze upon and that will remind me of him when I visit this chamber of memories."

"Khevan isn't dead," Twilka said. "And neither am I."

The Red Lady tilted her head, raising her eyebrows. "Soon enough."

"You're supposed to be testing him, not me. I'm only here to help."

"Khevan wants to leave my embrace to be with you. Are you worthy of such a sacrifice? I view that judgment as an integral part of the final challenge. I can't give him up to just anyone." The Lady strolled through an aisle of the macabre museum and Twilka reluctantly followed, clenching her hands so her nails dug into her palms. She hoped the slight pain would ward off the vertigo brought on by walking across what appeared to be the bottomless pit of a starfield.

Stopping to lift a long-stemmed flower and sniff it before rubbing the black petals against her cheek, the goddess said, "You did surprise me."

"When?"

"In the first moments of this challenge. You defeated two of your own worst fears. I expected one or the other to paralyze you until the time elapsed."

"Glad to disappoint you. I know we're limited on time for this challenge," Twilka said. "What is it you want me to do? And where's Khevan?"

"Where indeed?" The Lady spun in a slow circle, waving the flower like a wand. Glittering black sparks flew in all directions, winking out harmlessly. "He's here, if you can find him. After which, the two of you must win freedom by defeating warriors loyal to me."

Heart fluttering in her chest, Twilka stared at the nearest set of tables, which bore hundreds of items. Focusing on any one object in the clutter was a challenge. "I'll never be able to search this entire place, not if I had centuries."

"True. These are the Brothers I called mine over many millennia, so their number is endless. But finding Khevan is the first part of your challenge, daunting though the task may be for a mortal woman. You say you love him…"

"I do."

"Well then, let your heart lead you to him." The Red Lady laughed, the sound eerie, raising chills on Twilka's body. The goddess set the black rose on the edge of the table and faded from view, like a fire dying to embers until even the dark purple smoke dissolved.

"Lords of Space, we're in trouble, Khevan." Twilka shut her eyes for a moment, reopening them to scan the closest part of the collection, hoping something—anything—would attract her attention and serve as a red flag indicating here was her beloved.

No luck.

She wished she'd at least asked the Red Lady what exactly to search for. Even a non-answer might have provided a clue. Stomach in knots, she walked aimlessly in the direction the Lady had taken before she disappeared. Picking up an item at random here and there, before setting it carefully on the nearest cluttered surface, and moving a few more steps, she despaired. Speaking out loud to bolster her courage, she said, "How do I outthink an insane goddess? Khevan—or whatever she thinks reminds her of him—could be anywhere in this mess and her symbolic choice might mean nothing to me. I'll be trapped here myself if I don't figure out a strategy." Catching sight of herself reflected in a large silver mirror, Twilka shuddered and averted her eyes. "And I hate this damn dress." Talk about bad memories—the dress triggered memories of so many moments of terror, she could hardly stand the onslaught. For much of the last night on the *Nebula Dream*, she hadn't exactly covered herself with glory. Hopefully she'd atoned before the situation ended, but, "I am so not that version of myself anymore!"

The Red Lady had overwhelmed a more naïve Twilka in their encounter, later had stolen her man and her happiness. The dress symbolized the night and who she'd been. A reminder of her defeat when it came to keeping Khevan in her life.

Fists clenched, eyes shut tight, anger making her heart pound, Twilka said, "I should at least be able to pick my own clothing for this contest—does she have to control everything?"

When she moved, fabric swished against her ankles. "What the seven hells?" She gazed at herself in astonishment. No more midnight blue silk mini dress—now she wore the first dress she'd designed on Temple Home, the one she'd wanted to show Khevan, the one she was so proud of. The garment that launched her business. Fingering the fabric, she reminded herself once again, "Magic. This is all magic, all in my head."

Encouraged, she closed her eyes and tried to think only of Khevan. The loud ticking of an old fashioned chrono somewhere nearby distracted her, brought the awareness of the rapidly impending deadline racing to the surface, making chaos of her effort to concentrate only on the man she loved. "If I could find the damn clock, I'd smash it," she muttered. "Cheap trick, Red Lady." But effective.

Twilka turned to explore a different part of the collection and the annoying clock sat on a table right in front of her. A foot high and the same in length, it was a marvel of intricate gold filigree, set with rubies. An archaic round face displayed the time by means of a long and a short arrow, crossed, and a small pendulum below swung with each tick. Two tariqnas done in red enamel reared on either side of the clock face, framing it in their obsidian claws, and a solid gold figurine of a woman in a flowing, lowcut gown sat on the top, face modestly downcast as she carried a bouquet. Leaning closer, Twilka saw the woman was the Red Lady and the bouquet was actually an armful of knives with fancy ornamental hilts. Goose bumps rose on her arm. "That wasn't here a minute ago." *But I wished to find it and it came to me.*

Maybe I have more power here than I realize. She put her hand to her throat, where the small sun and star charm hung, suspended from a fine golden chain. The pendant represented the link between Khevan and herself, a pledge. Even the Red Lady's men acknowledged the fact. Mara had lent her the chain so she could wear the golden charm as a symbol. "Khevan, we're nearly out of time. Show me where you are, please."

She felt a tug on her hand, the one touching the necklace, as if he'd clasped it in his warm grip. Holding her breath, Twilka took a few tentative steps in the direction the invisible sensation seemed to be leading her. The pull became more powerful, as if an impatient companion wanted to drag her to a distant destination. She ran through the crowded room, swerving and dodging around the tables and shelves full of exotic items, until she stood in front of a series of black lacquered pedestals. The pull on her hand faded. Every square inch of the multi-level display was full of the Red Lady's disorganized bric-a-brac, but one statue, off to the side, nearly hidden behind other items drew Twilka's attention. Carefully, she moved a few pieces and lifted that one from the surface, stepping away from the table to better examine her prize.

A breathtaking bone china sculpture, the statue stood easily two feet tall, and depicted an ancient warrior clad in intricate battle armor, sword raised to strike a foe, shield on the other arm braced to defend the woman who rode at his back, arms circling his waist. The pair clung to a rearing black horse, mane and tail flying as it too screamed defiance at the invisible enemy. Rotating the statue, Twilka nearly dropped it.

The woman had her face.

Sinking to the floor, her knees losing all strength, Twilka set the statue on the floor. "I'm not dead, I'm not one of her worshippers. How *dare* she include me in her collection?" Hot with rage, she examined the piece further. The warrior was unmistakably Khevan, his strong, handsome features rendered perfectly, the scarlet tariqna tattoo spread across his cheek and forehead, its tail winding around his neck like a collar to disappear below the edge of the strange metal uniform. She touched the rider with her fingertips, caressing his shoulder. "All right, here we are, together. Now what?"

She'd hoped he'd magically appear once she found the right item, but nothing happened. She heard the infernal ticking again. The cursed clock had followed her and now sat on a nearby shelf, as if the timepiece was mocking her. Staring at the miniature Khevan, she whispered, "We have to get out of this creepy place."

Twilka spun the statue, racking her brain for a way to free her beloved and escape together.

Turning her palms up and cupping her hands as if in supplication, she willed the white tariqna to appear. It had never been of any use whatsoever in the past, but maybe here, in this uncanny place of power, the apparition could help. Hadn't the White Lady told Mara in her part of the *merdamier* challenge, she'd left one door open to possibility? Maybe this gift was the key. Within seconds, the creature manifested, sitting a few inches above her hands, wings wrapped protectively about its body, staring at her with baleful blue eyes. Twilka sighed. *Same as always, pretty but useless. Kind of the way I used to think of myself, wasn't it?* Until events on the *Nebula Dream* had shown her otherwise, opened her eyes to her own inner strength and potential.

"I need help," she said to the beast. "Why did the White Lady give you to me, if not to be helpful? I don't need cute souvenirs."

In the next moment she recoiled as the tariqna blinked, unfurled its iridescent wings, and rose into the air, hovering as it shifted its head from side to side, studying the surroundings. Twilka scrambled to her feet as the dragonlike beast expanded, becoming the size of a pony in the blink of an eye.

It's sure never done that before.

Head tilted, eyes glowing, the creature focused on the statue on the floor at her feet.

"No!" She grabbed for it, but the tariqna moved faster, capturing the figurine in its talons and flying away. Twilka ran to follow, cursing as she brushed past tables threatening to topple. She might hate the Red Lady, but she shrank from causing incidental damage by destroying the encapsulated memories of men and women who'd served her. Her quarrel lay with the goddess, not her people.

Well maybe she'd make an exception to destruction for Harbin, but he wasn't represented in this room, since he was still alive. *Too bad.*

The tariqna led her to the dais where she'd first arrived, hovering over the platform until Twilka nearly overtook the beast. Then, almost in slow motion, the creature opened its talons and let the statue fall. With a scream, she lunged onto the dais, but was too slow to catch the object, and the china shattered into a million pieces as it hit the black floor. Twilka sprawled on the pedestal, writhing in pain, as if by breaking the statue's representation of her, the tariqna had inflicted similar damage on the human model. Overwhelmed by the agony of all her nerve endings firing at once, she rolled onto her back and blacked out.

"Beloved, come back to me."

Khevan's deep voice penetrated the fog, enveloping her thoughts as he lifted her in his strong arms from the unforgiving floor, cradling her in his lap. She opened her eyes to stare into his handsome face, brow wrinkled in concern as he looked at her.

"I'm here," she said, raising one hand to cup his cheek, the one without the tattoo.

He crushed her to his chest and kissed her ferociously, bruising her lips with the force of his demand. Twilka wound her arms around his neck and clung as close as she could get to him, while sharing the passionate kiss. When the embrace ended, she rested her head on his broad chest, taking a moment to luxuriate in the reunion, but conscious they needed to be on the move.

"Where are we?" he said, raising his head and staring at their surroundings. "Why are we lying in a debris field? Were you hurling statuary at someone?"

"It's a long story."

The tariqna landed on the edge of the dais, folding its wings and shrinking to its former diminutive size before hopping to Twilka's outstretched hand like a pet bird.

Openmouthed, Khevan stared. "What is that?"

"A gift from the White Lady, the most useless present in the entire galaxy until today." She laughed as the tariqna lowered its head to stroke her hand before fading from view, blue eyes winking out last in an eerie manner. "I guess I needed the right occasion."

"Have you seen the Red Lady?" he asked. "How much time has elapsed in this challenge?"

"Yes, I've seen her and I've no idea how much time we've used up. She said once I found you we'd have to defeat her loyal warriors to gain our freedom." Swallowing hard, she said, "I guess that must be the mortal combat the Renegade described."

A loud ticking from the left of her signaled the arrival of the ancient clock, positioned just beyond the edge of the dais. "I should have asked the tariqna to drop *you*," she said, grabbing a jagged hunk of the china horse and throwing it at the clock. The fragment struck the timepiece a glancing blow, knocking it over. Although it fell with a metallic clang, the clock's malevolent ticking continued unabated.

Khevan grabbed her hand, pulling her close. "Don't worry; I've got you," he said directly into her ear. "I won't let you go until we're safe."

She laughed, clinging to him. "I've heard those words before."

"And I made good on the promise," he said, kissing her. Pulling back, he gazed into her eyes. "I'd been resigned to my fate, taking comfort in the fact of your safety." He laid a finger on her lips as she parted them to speak. "I didn't do you enough honor. You had more courage and resolve in your soul than I. When the Renegade told me you'd arrived on Temple Home determined to try to save me, and would participate in the ritual, I was angry. I didn't want you at risk after all I'd done and sacrificed to make you safe."

"Safety's highly overrated. Life is empty without you, nothing but a succession of days to get through," she said, running her hand through his hair. "I know that from the past five years I spent alone. This way we have a chance at a future together. Are you still angry?"

He nuzzled her neck, his voice a whisper. "Angry at him, not you. I thought he'd talked you into something foolish, perhaps failed to explain the heavy odds against us. Or burdened you with misplaced guilt."

"I take full ownership of my decisions," she said. "I didn't give anyone a chance to say no. We were on our way to you as soon as I recovered enough from Harbin's punch to think." She rubbed her jaw. "What comes next?"

"Combat is the final part of the ritual. I hope I get the chance to punish that bastard for hurting you." He glanced around the chamber. "But I can't imagine the Lady wanting us to fight here. Tell me about the white tariqna—can you summon it at will?"

"Usually, although it never got big before. Definitely a new trick."

"How did you acquire it?"

"That final day five years ago, when I was pining and waiting for you, and the head monk came to tell me to abandon hope and leave, I was in the White Lady's garden. He requested me to choose a pebble to take away, so to be polite, I did—I picked this pretty gray and white stone with a hint of sparkle. Then he closed my hand over it and when I uncurled my fingers a moment later, the stone was gone and the tariqna floated in the air over my palm. A good omen and a gift, said the monk, before he ushered me out to a waiting groundcar. I was driven to the spaceport, got onto my father's ship, and haven't been back to Temple Home again until we came to rescue you."

He touched her dress, rubbing the fabric between his fingers. "Pretty. Was this…"

"The one I made to show you? Yes. The Red Bitch brought me into this challenge in the dress from the *Nebula Dream*, can you imagine?" Twilka laughed. "Guess I showed her. What's going on? Why haven't we moved to the next phase?"

"She's stalling. Or she's trying to weaken me by allowing us time together, time to remember the stakes." He framed her face with his hands. "If I die, you die."

"We're not losing by default," Twilka said. Raising her voice, she yelled, "We're ready to get this over with. Bring on your D'nvannae assassins, Red Lady, so we can kick their asses and go home."

Khevan laughed. "You're crazy, but I love it."

"That's new." Twilka pointed. An elaborate red door, ornamented with golden tariqnas and other symbols, appeared in the blackness of space, obscuring some of the twinkling stars. The portal swung open, revealing a pastoral landscape beyond.

Khevan held out his hand. "The destination of the final battle. Shall we?"

Clasping his fingers, Twilka took a deep breath and made herself smile as she rose from the floor. "At least she isn't going to try throwing any more twisted vignettes from the *Dream* at us."

"Did she send you into your nightmare?" he asked as they walked arm in arm across the gleaming transparent floor to the door. "The one about the men outside the casino?"

Nodding, Twilka said, "I fought my way out of that moment. I bet I never have to dream it again."

"I feared she'd hit you with the memory, but I had no way to warn you. I'm proud of you for defeating her ploy. One's own fears are the worst demons."

"Oh, she wasn't done—she forced me to descend the gravlift on my own in order to find you. She tossed Harbin into the mix of problems as well, but he was mostly creepy and annoying."

"He'll probably be her champion, my opponent in the mortal combat, I warn you."

She pulled him to a halt right before crossing the threshold into the next part of the challenge, eyeing him up and down. "I wish you weren't going into this wearing her uniform and especially not carrying her brand. I think it's a disadvantage and messes with your mind. Makes you feel you still belong to her and are acting disloyal, instead of fighting for freedom." Twilka caressed his cheek with her hand. "I'd rather you went into battle free of her mark."

"Only she can remove the tariqna tattoo."

"Or maybe not." Twilka stared at his skin, where the scarlet mark was now smeared and faded wherever she'd touched it. She dragged him to the side, to another table where a mirrorlike shield leaned precariously against some abstract crystal sculptures. "See what I was able to do?"

Tilting his head and moving it from side to side, eyes narrowed, he studied the now defaced symbol. "Interesting. I wouldn't have expected this. You may be right about the symbolism." Tentatively, he rubbed at the tattoo.

Twilka caught his hand. "Don't! When you touch it the red becomes more prominent." Pulling on his shoulder, she said, "Bend down a bit; let me try something." She gathered her skirt and rubbed the fabric gently on his cheek. Wherever she touched, the tattoo disappeared. Laughing in delight, she said, "See, you do belong to me. Well, to us." She wiped his neck, obliterating the collarlike tail portion of the marking, which had always bothered her.

"Impressive. Any other last minute ideas? Because now we're the ones delaying and could be declared the losers."

With fumbling fingers, she unclasped the golden chain and put the pendant around his neck. "Only this. Our personal contract, okay?"

"Okay." He touched her lips with his for a fleeting kiss. "Time to go." He took her hand and escorted her gallantly through the door.

Twilka found herself standing on a large dais with two round platforms next to each other and a rectangle outlined on the pavement in red. It was night, although the sky was lightening in the east. Barely showing above the western horizon, a large, pockmarked moon illuminated the scene. The dais was in a meadow, with a stream meandering close by, and oddly shaped trees growing in clusters here and there. "Are we on her home planet?"

"Perhaps, although the legend among the Brotherhood says the sisters' original home is long gone, destroyed by a supernova, so this is most likely an illusion like all the rest. There's the fighting ground," Khevan said, pointing at the painted area. "I must stand there to await my opponent."

"How do you know?"

"This resembles our primary training areas, where hand-to-hand killing skills are taught."

"Where do I go?"

Before he could answer her question, there was a sizzling sound, as if the air was burning, followed by a roar of thunder and the glare of a lightning strike.

"Here, girl." The Red Lady, draped in her flowing scarlet dress, now sat semi-reclined on a large couch, flames dancing and cavorting all around. She gestured at the couch in the center of the empty platform beside her. "You may use my sister's dais, since she won't be joining us tonight."

Twilka stared at her for a moment, gauging the risk of accepting the assigned location. The longer she focused on the other woman, the more the figure of the Lady blurred and she thought she saw something larger, misshapen, alien, bathed in the fire. She shivered.

"The Lady isn't human, remember." Khevan's whisper was nearly inaudible as he squeezed her hand. "She takes the human form most often because our civilization is primarily made up of humanoids, but you must never think of her as being one of us." He removed his jacket, shirt and boots, dropping them onto the ground, and prepared to step into the designated area barefoot, turning to Twilka at the last moment. "A kiss for luck?"

Choking on sudden tears of fright for him, refusing to let him see her terror, Twilka smiled and raised her face to his. "We'll be free soon."

He brushed a kiss across her lips before crossing the red line, taking a stance, and launching into stylized preliminary warm up moves, his body shifting smoothly from one position into the next, the speed of motion increasing. In any other circumstances, she'd enjoy watching him.

Twilka walked to the empty raised circle, but paused at the last moment. Taking a place where a goddess should sit didn't feel right. "I'm not your sister. I think I'll watch from over here, thanks all the same."

"Suit yourself," the Red Lady said, as Twilka strolled to a nearby broken pillar and sat on the edge.

"I usually do." She had the sensation she'd avoided some kind of trap, although in this deadly game they were playing, nothing was cut and dried.

Harbin emerged from the closest grove of trees and bounded onto the platform, wearing a red robe, which he discarded to reveal he was bare to the waist, displaying sculpted muscles as defined and impressive as Khevan's, clad only in the order's trademark black leather pants. He bowed to the Red Lady and then gave Twilka a sarcastic salute. "I'll enjoy killing you, once I've disposed of our traitor."

"She's not your problem—I am," Khevan said in a harsh voice. "Are you here to talk and give offense, or to fight and prove your worth?"

Kicking off the sandals he'd worn, Harbin stepped into the rectangle. "First man to set foot outside the line, even by a toe, loses. Otherwise, the fight is to the death, no mercy asked or given." He turned his head to stare at Twilka. "And no interference or the match is forfeit."

Raising her eyebrows, she met and held his challenging stare. Pointing her index finger at the Red Lady, she said, "As long as the rule applies to both of us."

The goddess didn't deign to respond. She waved a lazy hand. "Let the match begin."

Somewhere a gong sounded, the booming note echoing in the quiet morning air.

Twilka gasped as the two men begin circling each other in a deadly ceremonial dance with precise steps, sizing each other up, jabbing and moving away with amazing speed. The sheer fluidity of the moves inspired awe. Constantly in motion, constantly testing each other. Both were protecting their ribs as much as possible and using the strength of their entire bodies as power behind the blows, especially those made with the legs. Khevan drew first blood, launching a kick whose impact rocked Harbin, although he fell away from the ferocity of the blow, somersaulted, and rose to retaliate with his own.

Khevan parried, slipping aside as Harbin's flurry of strikes came at him, then grabbing his opponent and throwing him to the surface. Quick as a snake, Harbin whipped his legs and, even though Khevan danced aside, he fell as Harbin managed to trip him. Springing to his feet before his opponent could capitalize on the momentary weakness, Khevan settled into his fighting stance again. The two men danced around each other before Harbin struck. The next set of blows came, each man striking, bobbing and weaving so fast Twilka's head spun. Harbin feinted and landed a solid blow on Khevan's left ribcage. Although the impact looked and sounded terrifying to Twilka, Khevan danced away. The men engaged again in another sequence of blows. Khevan managed to catch the final strike and land his own blow at Harbin's neck, although partially blocked, and followed with a three punch combination. Clearly, the Red Lady's champion was shaken, dropping to one knee.

A gong sounded.

"Knives," the Red Lady said.

Twilka recognized Khevan's red handled, golden-bladed knives as the weapons materialized on the platform. Another set, which Harbin grabbed, cockily tossing one in the air and snatching it as it fell, were equally menacing. Khevan advanced on Harbin immediately, driving the other man toward the red line. He drew first blood, scoring a long slash across Harbin's ribcage before his enemy mounted a belated defense and deflected the follow-up blow.

Twilka swallowed hard as the combat continued, the flurry of blows too fast to follow. After one encounter, blood flowed freely in a scarlet ribbon down Khevan's side, and she realized Harbin must have penetrated his defenses at least once. Harbin appeared to her to be on the defensive, mostly using his weapons to keep Khevan from scoring hits, while getting in very few stabs or slashes of his own. Harbin's features were set in a look of intense concentration, eyes narrowed, teeth clenched. Sweat glistened on his face and torso. Khevan's face was serene and confident, his gaze locked onto Harbin as if assessing the other man and finding him sadly lacking. There was no denying the amount of energy this death match was consuming, but Khevan moved as fluidly as ever, showing no sign of weariness. Twilka herself was tense, body taut as a bowstring, hands fisted as she watched her lover fight for both of their lives.

Khevan danced in close and used the butt of one knife as an impact weapon, landing a blow to Harbin's chin and stabbing him with the blade in the other hand. Harbin retreated to the far end of the rectangle, Khevan following, constantly jabbing and attacking, aiming at different parts of his opponent's body. As the match went on, Twilka admired the way Khevan stayed in control, moving in sync with Harbin, who was clearly beginning to panic as he realized how overmatched he was.

Khevan was going to drive Harbin out of the rectangle and win without the necessity for killing the man in front of her. Twilka began to relax as the outcome of his strategy became obvious to her. He was within seconds of securing the victory when the Lady's command and the sound of the gong startled her.

"Stand down!"

As the sound of the gong reverberated, Khevan took a final slash, aiming at Harbin's neck. His opponent fell in a heap, one hand falling outside the red rectangle.

"I claim the victory," Khevan said, wheeling to face the Lady. "I've won my freedom."

"Oh, no." Her voice was a purr, low and menacing. "You've managed to defeat the first Brother I sent against you, true. Clearly not the man worthy of ascending and claiming your previous place at my side, unable to back up his promises to me with adequate skill. But the challenge isn't over."

Khevan straightened and Twilka gasped as four more hulking D'nvannae marched out of the grove onto the platform, forming a line beside the Lady's throne.

"How is this fair?" Twilka said, fury rising inside her. "He's already fought."

"But you have not. Time for you to cease playing the spectator and take your place by his side. That's what you want, isn't it?"

"Not in the ring of combat!" Khevan strode as close as he could get without leaving the contest area. "She's not a trained warrior. You make a mockery of this challenge, forcing a non-initiate to stand against four highly lethal Brothers. I protest."

"The essence of this schism between you and me as your Lady involves her. Deny it if you can. Had you never met her, or become involved with her, you would have served me honorably all your days. She is the problem." The Lady's voice was angry, yet persuasive. "For the final time, I make you an offer—renounce this human woman and reclaim your place at my side. Rank, privileges—all will be restored. She'll be released from my temple unharmed. The pleasures of *tazlin* in my flames can be yours again within the hour and I'll ensure you forget her. There'll be no hidden memories this time."

Twilka held her breath. She trusted Khevan with all her heart, but he'd succumbed to the Red Lady's pressure once before in an attempt to save her life.

Khevan stared at her for a heart stopping moment, his gaze intense. Then he swung to address the Lady. "Twilka and I agree there is no life without each other. Better we leave this world now, together, than endure another separation." He wheeled, holding out his hand to Twilka. "I'm sorry our fate has come to this, but will you join me?"

"Of course." Twilka could barely force herself to walk toward the combat ring. The four D'nvannae executioners were stripping to the waist, each more heavily muscled than the next. She couldn't stand against these bruisers in any sort of a physical contest, much less one involving knives. Khevan wouldn't be able to go on the offensive or protect himself because he'd be frantic to save her. *Clever trap, Red Lady.*

Cool silk whispered across her body, replacing the smooth feel of the knit dress she'd been wearing. Glancing down, Twilka saw the goddess had seen fit to clothe her in the cursed midnight blue dress again. *Oh, hell no.* Stopping in mid-step, thoughts racing, she addressed the Lady. "I have no experience with knives."

"Are you rethinking your part in this tragedy? Do you wish to withdraw?" Eyes wide, the goddess appeared intrigued. "I might be persuaded, if you grovel sufficiently."

Twilka shook her head. "No, I've agreed to the combat at my lover's side. I merely request to be allowed to use my own skills and weapons, since I can't wield a knife." Forcing a small laugh, she added, "Except to carve my steak."

The Red Lady assessed her. "You may employ whatever is within you, whatever tactics and skills you do possess, which I'm sure are minimal. If you have a weapon, you may deploy it."

"And no more tricks? No more of this last second 'oh, wait a minute, there's another twist to this challenge' stuff? Once we've defeated your four men, these four men standing here, we're free to go?"

"Bargaining with me is not generally a good idea," the Lady said, her voice deep and clipped. There was an odd echo, as if thunder murmured in the distance.

"I'm merely seeking to clarify the terms."

"The human is within her rights." The Chief Monk of the White Lady's order stood on the dais which had been empty. He leaned on his staff. "What she has requested is fair." He straightened and pointed his gnarled staff at the horizon. "Best hurry, the moon has nearly set and the sun prepares to rise." Now he gave Twilka a meaningful look. "At the first ray of dawn, the contest ends."

"I'm ready." As she prepared to take the final step across the red line to join Khevan, she concentrated fiercely, visualizing herself in her own dress. Between one step and the next, as her foot fell inside the rectangle, she felt herself swathed in the cotton again and didn't bother to hide her satisfaction or the grin on her face.

Clearly puzzled, brow furrowed, Khevan didn't ask any questions. Taking her hand, he drew her toward the far end of the ring, away from Harbin's body. "Do you want a knife?"

She shook her head. "No, thanks."

"Stand behind me—they'll have to kill me to get at you. It will but delay the inevitable…"

Twilka rested her hand on his arm. "It'll be fine; trust me."

He took her in his arms, gazing at her face. "I regret bringing you to this moment, to this death, but I regret nothing else about us."

She went on tiptoes to kiss him. "Don't give up too soon."

"The match is about to begin," said the Lady. "Are you ready?"

Twilka stepped away from Khevan, to stand at his side, not behind him. "We are."

The four Brothers filed into the rectangle, spreading out in a semi-circle, ringing Khevan and her. Knives out, faces set in stern lines, eyes glittering, the quartet assumed offensive stances, blades raised.

Laughing, Twilka cupped her hands in front of her, at chest height. "Appear!"

The white tariqna materialized, growing from kitten-size to taller than Twilka in the blink of an eye. Wings extended, blue eyes glowing balefully, hovering at Twilka's side, the creature spun in midair to face the D'nvannae.

"What trickery is this? My sister can't intervene to help you now—meddling by her is forbidden." The Red Lady's protest was immediate and shrill.

Tossing her head, ferocious and giddy, Twilka stared straight at the goddess and said, "She gave me this gift a long time ago, when you stole Khevan and imprisoned him, in fact. You agreed I could use whatever was within me. Well *this* is what I bring to the battle."

The blindingly white tariqna extended its snakelike neck, opened its beak wide, and bugled a challenge.

"The conditions were agreed to; the match is fair." The white monk swung his staff and struck the gong. "Begin."

The four Brothers exchanged dubious glances.

The tariqna launched itself in a deadly attack, grabbing the nearest man in its razor sharp talons, throwing him aside in a bloody heap a moment later. The three remaining assassins separated, trying to surround the tariqna as it worried at the body of its first victim. Plunging his knife deep into the creature's back, at the base of the left wing, the largest warrior yelled a curse. Shrieking its pain and displeasure, the tariqna snaked its neck to seize the enemy in its beak. As the Brother tried to stab the dripping knife into the nearest glowing blue eye, the tariqna flew straight upward, bringing its claws into play to snatch its assailant from the platform. With one violent move, the creature sliced its prey nearly in two and dropped him like a child's doll. He hit the stone platform and lay unmoving, neck broken. The two remaining D'nvannae retreated, but not before one snatched their dead companion's blade, shoving it into his belt.

Knives flashing, Khevan strode forward and sought to engage them in combat. Distracted by the hovering tariqna, the first man was easily vanquished, falling with a stab wound to the chest and a slashed neck. Twilka advanced, the tariqna flying protectively above her head, and stood beside Khevan again.

The fourth man cursed and lunged forward, blade in reverse hold, stabbing at Twilka's heart. Khevan threw himself between them, his body shielding hers, and the attacker buried his knife to the hilt in Khevan's side. Screaming, Twilka grabbed a knife from Khevan's hand as he fell and stood protectively over him.

The Brother drew himself upright and stepped back, grabbing the extra knife from his belt and saluting her with the bloodstained blade. "What now? Will you have your creature kill me? Take the easy way out? No blood on *your* hands but the stain of cowardice on your heart. Or do you have the guts to fight for your life and Khevan's?" Throwing his arms out in a grandiose gesture, he swiveled his head to the avidly watching goddess. "I'll even let her land the first blow, before I kill her for you, my Lady."

Twilka didn't hesitate for a moment, jumping over Khevan, taking the Brother by surprise. More by pure luck than anything else, she knocked his knife hand aside with her left arm and went for his eyes with her clawed right hand. Astonished and off balance, he fell, Twilka on top of him. She pinned his arm with her own body weight, continuing to target his eyes, scratching and gouging at his face like a madwoman, screaming defiance. She knew she'd won only a fleeting victory and could feel him gathering his strength to throw her aside, even as he tried to ward off her attack. Operating from sheer instinct mixed with terror, she brought her left hand up and slashed the D'nvanne's neck with Khevan's knife. Eyes wide in astonishment, hand to his gushing artery, the Brother rolled away from her. Twilka staggered to her feet, dropping the knife and covering her mouth to avoid throwing up at the sight of the scarlet blood pooling on the stone.

She averted her gaze from the dying man's staring eyes and turned to Khevan.

"Can you stand?" Twilka pulled at his arm.

"To finish this? Yes."

Together, with him leaning so heavily on Twilka she nearly fell, they faced the Lady and the monk. "We've won your challenge," he said as the first rays of the sun burst over the horizon and illuminated the scene.

The White Monk thumped his staff on the platform and pointed one hand at the Red Lady. "The victory is theirs. Release him from his oath, remove his tattoo, and banish him from your order, a free man. Relinquish any hold or hatred you bear the woman. This couple is your concern no longer."

Twilka could hardly bear to look at the Red Lady, no longer a thing of beauty, but a misshapen alien figure, tentacles and forked tail lashing. The flames obscured the details, but Twilka was sure she'd have newly spawned nightmares forever if she could see what occupied the couch.

The goddess's voice remained as beautiful as ever, however, even filled with rage. "Very well. I declare you both free of all connection with me forever more. Leave my presence and know it will mean instant death if ever you return."

The white tariqna bugled and flew straight into the rays of the rising sun, vanishing in a blaze of rainbow-colored flares.

A pulse of red flame came at her so quickly Twilka couldn't move to avoid it, but although heat washed over her body, she took no other harm.

CHAPTER TEN

She found herself standing locked in Khevan's arms in the ruby-lined fire pit, in the now empty and dark *merdamier* chamber. The Renegade leaned against the wall, smiling at them, and the White Monk stood beside the pit, his demeanor calm as ever.

"We're done? We're safe?" she said. "No more tests?"

"Together, you have triumphed," the Monk answered. "Let us depart this place."

Khevan assisted her in climbing from the pit, then went to one knee beside her, retaining his grip on her hand. "I give you my oath now, for the rest of my life and beyond. There will only ever be you in my heart. I will gladly die to defend you and I want nothing more than to stand at your side."

She moistened her dry and cracked lips. "If you just issued a marriage proposal, the answer is yes."

He rose, catching her in his arms and swinging her in a circle as they kissed.

The Renegade cleared his throat. "My congratulations and felicitations, but best we leave now, as the Monk suggested. The Red Lady gave her word, but she can be capricious. None of us want to give her any excuse to embark on a fresh vendetta."

"Words of wisdom." Khevan set Twilka carefully on her feet, taking her hand, and the four of them left the empty chamber. The monk led the way through the dark corridor, the tip of his staff glowing with a diffused white light.

"How did you know what to do when the last Brother challenged you?" Khevan asked Twilka, his voice low and meant only for her. "My heart stopped when you ran forward, I swear. I thought I was going to witness your death and instead you triumphed."

She laughed even as she shivered. "Pure gut instinct. He was so busy strutting for the Red Lady that I saw my chance and caught him off guard. I was hoping either you or the tariqna would jump in and help me out…"

"But you didn't need either of us." He hugged her close.

"I-I can't believe I killed someone with my own hands." She glanced at her palms, unable to see clearly in the dimly lit hall, but there was no blood. "He is dead, isn't he? And Harbin, and the others?"

Khevan shrugged. "Who can say? If you or I—or Nick—had died in the Red Lady's challenges, yes, we'd have perished in real life as well. Those were the stakes we agreed to. She might not actually sacrifice her own people."

"I really want creepy Harbin to be dead." Swallowing hard, she asked, "Does that make me an awful person?"

"She will have been extremely displeased at their failure to defeat you," the Renegade said quietly. "Harbin in particular had much to lose. I wouldn't worry over it. Her men made their choices, as did Khevan."

Twilka came to an abrupt halt, realizing the White Lady's monk had paused at the massive front door of the building. Hand on the intricately carved knob, their elderly escort turned to give them a measuring stare. "Try to leave the experiences of the night behind you. Declare yourselves free of the Red Lady, even as she has cast you from her mind. You want no ties between you."

"You give good advice, sir," Khevan said, making a half bow. "Some memories are harder to erase than others." He squeezed Twilka's hand as the monk nodded and swung the door open.

Twilka took a deep breath and crossed the threshold, hand in hand with Khevan, emerging into the fresh, clear morning sunlight outside.

Nick and Mara rose from the bench where they'd been waiting, guarded by the monks of the White Lady's order.

"Are we ever glad to see the two of you!" Nick gave them a searching glance as Mara and Twilka exchanged hugs. "You both look worn out, to say the least. We free and clear now?"

Khevan nodded. "It's done, I'm no longer a D'nvannae." He put a hand to his brow. "I don't know what I am, having been in the Brotherhood since I was a boy of eight."

"We'll figure it out," Twilka said, patting his arm. "We're going to be married," she informed the others.

"I can perform the ceremony today," said the Monk. "In the Lady of Light's garden. That much delay is permitted and it will be an auspicious beginning to your life together. Then you must be on your way. Never set foot on this planet again." Arms outstretched, wielding his staff like a crook, he tried to shepherd them in the direction of his goddess's temple.

"Will you stand with me?" Khevan asked Nick as the group began walking.

"Proud to do the duty," he said. "Much easier to do than watching your six in the *merdamier*! And later, on my ship, we can discuss the future, as far as what's next. I think you've got the skill set to fit right in with my private security firm. You'd make an excellent partner."

"Nick tends to be a bit hot headed," Mara said with a laugh. "You might be able to inject some badly needed caution into the planning."

Khevan stopped in the middle of the square. "I want to thank all of you for coming to stand with me against the Red Lady, for risking yourselves on my behalf."

Twilka stretched out her hand and Mara clasped it, Nick laying his on top of theirs. Khevan leaned forward to join the embrace.

"We've all been living on borrowed time since the *Nebula Dream*," Nick said, "And we only survived that experience and this one because we have each other's sixes. We're a good team."

"Literally forged in fire now," Twilka agreed. "Nothing can break us apart or come between us. If the Red Lady of D'nvannae couldn't do it, with all her wiles and tricks, nothing can."

The Chief Monk said, "We'd best be proceeding with the wedding you requested me to perform. I don't want you lingering on Temple Home too long, tempting fate. The victory you won last night is rare, not repeatable."

They followed him toward the elaborate edifice of the White Lady's complex, gleaming in the bright sunshine.

Nick dug a com out of his pants pocket. "I'm going to give Rafferty a heads up to be ready for departure on a moment's notice."

"Too bad he and Casey can't be at the wedding," Twilka said, her steps slowing a bit.

"No time," the Renegade told her as she mounted the steps to enter the temple. "Casey can be baking you a wedding cake in his ship's fancy galley to console himself for missing the ceremony itself."

Mara linked arms with Twilka. "Where do you want us to take you for the honeymoon? Any ideas?"

"Anywhere—I'm not choosy, as long as Khevan is there…" She broke off, realizing her lover had stopped a few stairs below her. Leaving Mara, she went to join him, resting her hand on his arm. "What's the matter?"

He shook his head and gave her a dazzling smile. "Nothing. I thought I heard drums for an instant."

Twilka held her breath. "Did they—did she tempt you?"

Khevan glanced over his shoulder at the D'nvannae temple. "Not even for a moment." He turned to Twilka. "I'm well and truly free of her."

"You'll never escape *my* clutches," she said, going on tiptoe to kiss him.

"Our friends are waiting," he murmured as he held her close. "And people are beginning to stare."

"I don't care—I want everyone to see how happy I am on my wedding day." But, keeping her tight hold on his hand, she turned to climb the rest of the stairs.

Nick and the others had apparently gone ahead inside, as the space by the beautifully carved doors was empty. The portal stood open.

As she reached the entrance and stepped across the threshold into the space beyond, Twilka was enveloped in a cloud of indescribably intoxicating perfume and a bright white light surrounded them. Dimly, she was aware of the door closing behind her.

"Well done," said a voice in tones as musical as crystals chiming. "On occasion it serves my sister a good lesson to lose something or someone. Yours was a hard fought victory and all the sweeter for that."

Her vision clearing as the incandescent light dimmed a bit, Twilka found herself facing a breathtakingly beautiful woman clad all in white robes, her long blonde hair floating around her, a diadem of iridescent stars for a crown. A large white tariqna crouched on either side, wings folded along their spines, bright blue eyes gleaming as they studied the humans.

Khevan bowed his head and went down on one knee. "You honor us, my Lady. I was sure I'd never see you again."

She laughed and the sound was enchanting. "And I am pleased you've chosen to marry in my garden."

"Thank you for the help," Twilka said. "My tariqna and the senior monk…"

The Lady in White inclined her head gracefully. "Khevan was meant to be one of mine, long ago, before life took twists and turns. I was moved to assist by the memory of his mother's gentle spirit."

A little alarmed by the possessive sound of the first remark, Twilka opened her mouth to protest. White Lady or not, she wasn't about to lose Khevan now.

The goddess raised one hand and seemed to be suppressing a smile. "Calm yourself, child, I have no claim on him whatsoever. I rejoice that he's found his way to you." She stood aside, pointing to an arch on the far wall. "My monk waits to marry you, so I'll delay you no longer. My blessings upon you both."

Khevan rose and turned to Twilka. "I have no ring to give you. I was in such haste."

Clearing her throat, the goddess said, "I've taken care of the lack."

Twilka stared at her, then at her gracefully outstretched hand, where two plain golden rings nestled beside a third more intricately carved band.

Khevan plucked the latter from goddess's palm and took Twilka's left hand, sliding the cool band onto her ring finger. She stretched her arm and turned the ring this way and that, admiring the exquisite workmanship of the tiny platinum tariqna, curled nose to tail around her finger, sparkling blue stones set for eyes.

"Does this one…"

"Come to life?" The goddess laughed. "No. This is only a ring, forged from metal mined on my home world long ago. A token of my affection and my blessing. The two of you have been a most interesting episode in my long life." She dropped the pair of golden bands into Khevan's hand. "Your friends await your arrival to the ceremony my monk has offered to perform."

Khevan took Twilka's hand and she did her best to curtsey, pulling on very old memories of a childhood dance class, feeling some sign of respect was called for, but having no idea what a goddess might expect. She allowed her lover to draw her away toward the arch that led to the garden, but took one final glance back at the Lady in White, so different from her sister.

The goddess was gone, as if she'd never been there to greet them. Golden motes of dust floated in a shaft of early morning sunshine.

Nick met them at the arch. "Where have you two been? We were getting worried the Red Lady might have changed her mind." His tone of voice suggested he was at least half serious.

"I needed a ring," Khevan said. "The issue has been remedied. We're ready."

Nick gave him a quizzical look. "It's the best man's job to hold the rings. Hand them over."

Mara joined them, offering Twilka a fragrant bouquet of the local flowers, all in vivid colors, the combined scent not unlike the perfume of the White Lady herself. "The monk allowed me to pick these—he even suggested a few blooms. I think he's enjoying this rare occasion. Shall I walk you down the aisle?" She gave Nick a small push. "You two go join the monk and wait for us."

"Yes, ma'am." Grinning, Nick bent to brush a kiss over her lips before he pulled Khevan away, stepping into the garden.

Alone with her friend for a moment, Twilka raised the stunning bouquet to her nose and took a deep breath. Fingering the petals of one particularly gorgeous purple flower, she said, "I don't know that I ever expected to actually marry anyone. Kind of an unusual step for a Socialite like me. We either stay single or we have a Sectors-wide blowout and spend a lot of daddy's money, you know?" She gave Mara a sideways glance. "Then get divorced a year or two later and move on."

Mara hugged her, careful not to crush the flowers. "But you do want to proceed? Because we can stop the ceremony…"

"I want this more than I've ever wanted anything in my entire life. I mean, after what we've been through, nothing can separate Khevan and me ever again, but he's a very traditional guy under all that sexy black leather, apparently. And, to my surprise, I think I am too. Who knew?" She grinned, admiring the tariqna ring coiled around her finger. "His proposal after *merdamier* ended was breathtaking. I even have an engagement ring, courtesy of the Lady in White. Hey, I can use this as inspiration for a new line of wedding attire."

"All right, I've seen that look on your face before." Taking her elbow and adjusting Twilka's hair ever so slightly, Mara drew her forward. "No designing until after the ceremony and we're safely off the planet. Let's go get you married."

About to make some witty quip in reply, Twilka raised her eyes and saw Khevan waiting at the far end of the garden, in the very spot where she'd cried her eyes out after he disappeared from her life five years ago. Nick and the Renegade flanked him and a small group of hastily assembled monks were off to the side, singing to the accompaniment of a flute and what looked like a violin.

Khevan had evidently been watching for her and his face lit up in an unaccustomed, huge smile as she and Mara walked along the path toward the small group, timing their steps to the rhythm of the monk choir's lilting music.

As the song ended, Mara squeezed Twilka's hand before transferring it to Khevan's, whose grip crushed her fingers.

"Relax," she stage whispered, leaning toward him. "We've got this."

"There is no life without you," he said.

The senior monk cleared his throat. "I have the proper words to recite, if you'd like to continue this ceremony in the accepted fashion." The twinkle in his eye belied the stern tone. "I realize you need no vows, no blessing from me, to seal the bond between you, but as we stand in the Lady's garden, let us proceed."

Twilka handed the bouquet to Mara so she could grasp both of Khevan's hands. The ceremony was quick and she knew she'd barely remember the words she'd spoken later, but when the monk pronounced them united, Khevan swept her into his arms for a kiss that seemed to go on forever while their friends cheered, the monks sang, and a flight of white tariqnas flew an intricate pattern overhead, weaving through sparkling bursts of color in the sky.

"The White Lady isn't subtle, is she?" Safe in Khevan's arms, Twilka stared at the display overhead in the morning sky. "Will her sister be upset? I love it, but the display does seem like a pointed jab."

"Your new wife is correct," the Renegade said. "Far be it from me to criticize either goddess, but I think you should be going. Now."

"Ordinarily, I'd provide a feast and order more songs in your honor from my chorus. Your friends would offer toasts." The Senior Monk appeared a bit sad as he contemplated the festivities that would have to be foregone. "But your groundcar awaits you at the rear of the temple."

"I've told Rafferty to be ready to lift off the moment we arrive," Nick said, bending to kiss Twilka on the cheek. "You made a beautiful bride, kid."

Clutching her bouquet, Twilka said a hurried thank you to the monk before Khevan and her friends swept her away, hastening through the halls of the White Lady's temple behind a young brother who radiated excitement at all the unusual occurrences.

True to the monk's promise, a groundcar was waiting, engine revving.

They piled in and the driver took off almost before the door was shut, heading for the spaceport beyond the ancient city. The Renegade remained behind, standing on the temple steps, watching them pull away.

Twilka leaned into Khevan's embrace and took another deep breath of the flowers' perfume before gazing into his eyes. "This reminds me of the last time I left Temple Home, except today is so much better, to be leaving free and clear with you."

"I regret the time we lost," he said, his voice low, the words meant for her ears alone.

She shook her head. "I think we had to take a winding path to this point, to really appreciate what we've won."

"Surviving the wreck of the *Nebula Dream* was enough to bind Nick and Mara forever," he said.

"We're more complicated. But I like that about us, now that the waiting, the loneliness, and the battle is over." She pulled him closer for a kiss.

"No regrets?"

Twilka shook her head, stroking his cheek, now bare of any tattoo or mark. He captured her hand, dropping a tender kiss on her ring finger.

"I did forget to ask the monk to add one thing to the wedding vows."

Head tilted, he gazed at her with a smile. "And what might that be?"

"Considering everything we've been through, starting with the *Nebula Dream* and up through today, I want a promise from you that our future will never be boring. We've set a high standard now and you know we Socialites can't stand to be bored." She felt giddy with the pleasure of being together finally, no obstacles standing between them and the life she craved with Khevan. Teasing him just added to the fun.

His laugh filled the groundcar, startling Nick and Mara, who'd been having their own private conversation in the front.

"I assure you, my beautiful bride, no moment of a life with you will be boring."

"Good."

"Although anyone made of less stern stuff than you might request some peace and quiet," he said with a sly grin.

She shook her head although she was laughing. "That's a deal breaker for me, non-negotiable."

"Consider the issue moot, not worthy of another thought. And just in case this sedate car ride is beginning to bore you…" He hit the privacy screen button, obscuring the view of their seats from the car's other occupants and gathered her close. "Allow me to demonstrate my good intentions."

***

Thank you for reading STAR SURVIVORS!

Don't miss the first book in the connected series:
ESCAPE FROM ZULAIRE

Andi Markriss hasn't exactly enjoyed being the house guest of the planetary high-lord, but her company sent her to represent them at a political wedding. When hotshot space marine Captain Tom Deverane barges in on the night of the biggest social event of the summer, Andi isn't about to offend her high-ranking host on Deverane's say-so—no matter how sexy he is, or how much he believes they need to leave now.

Deverane was thinking about how to spend his retirement bonus when HQ assigned him one last mission: rescue a civilian woman stranded on a planet on the verge of civil war. Someone has pulled some serious strings to get her plucked out of the hot zone. Deverane's never met anyone so hard-headed—or so appealing. Suddenly his mission to protect this one woman has become more than just mere orders.

That mission proves more dangerous than he expected when rebel fighters attack the village and raze it to the ground. Deverane escapes with Andi--barely.

On their hazardous journey through the wilderness, Andi finds herself fighting her uncomfortable attraction to the gallant and courageous captain. But Deverane's not the type to settle down, and running for one's life doesn't leave much time for romance.

Then Andi is captured by the rebel fighters, but Deverane has discovered that Zulaire's so-called civil war is part of a terrifying alien race's attempt to subjugate the entire Sector. If he pushes on to the capitol, Andi will die. Deverane must decide whether to save the woman he loves, or sacrifice her to save Zulaire.

Please enjoy this excerpt from Escape from Zulaire

The Sectors Special Forces captain awaiting Andi in the library stood with his back to the door, hands on his hips, staring at one of Lord Tonkiln's prized abstract paintings. Well over six feet of hard warrior, he'd rolled his camouflage uniform sleeves up, revealing muscular arms matching the rest of his physique. Andi glimpsed the hint of an intriguing tattoo, a black sword wreathed in comets, on one bicep. His hair was sandy brown, a bit shaggy for military correctness. He tapped the toe of his boot against the expensive mahogany floor. The captain's whole attitude suggested a man poised for decisive action at a moment's notice, reinforced by the way he wheeled at the sound of the door opening.

"Finally." His glance at the military chrono on his tanned wrist was an unconscious gesture of annoyance at time forever lost.

Green eyes in a tanned, ruggedly handsome face. Andi's knees went a little wobbly for a moment. *My particular weakness in a man.* Classic square jaw, straight nose, high forehead with a small scar on his cheek.

His eyebrows drew together in a frown. "Miss Markriss?"

"Why are you here?" Andi snapped out of her fascination with his features, feeling her cheeks grow hot. *Wow, was I blatantly staring or what?* "Has something happened to Dave Flintmay? The Loxton planetary agent?"

Flashing very white teeth in that tanned face, he smiled at her, but the too-easy grin didn't reach his tired eyes. "Don't you people get the news out here? Comlinks broken?"

She blinked, trying to follow this unexpected conversation starter. "What?"

Lady Tonkiln received a stack of messages each morning, from either her husband or friends in the capital. Lysanda also had many messages, filled with inconsequential social gossip. Nothing for Andi, but then, everyone knew she was on an extended vacation from the office. The Loxton operation was on its summer hiatus along with most of Zulaire. "Of course we get news. What does that have to do with anything? Captain, what are you *doing* here?"

Glancing at Iraku, the officer's lips tightened as if he bit back some hasty comment. Unabashedly eavesdropping, the Naranti servant remained by the open door. "Thank you, I think the lady and I can manage."

Andi stifled a laugh. The gardener's assistant had been right—the captain's accent was pretty bad, soft on the consonants and missing the required prefixes. *His hypnotraining must have been a rush job.*

Iraku stared at the outworlder, who glared back, jaw clenched, one hand resting on the butt of his blaster.

I never tried outright dismissal on the old dictator. Avoiding him sure doesn't work. Breaking the silence, Andi tried for a gracious note. "Thanks for escorting me, Iraku. Can you do me a favor and inform Lady Tonkiln I've returned to the house, since she was concerned?" Blinking at last, the servant bowed low. He left without another word but drew the door closed behind him in a leisurely fashion calculated to infuriate the impatient captain.

As Andi watched in disbelief, Deverane crossed to the door. Opening it a few inches, he checked to be sure Iraku hadn't lingered within earshot, before shutting the door again.

Offering no explanation to Andi for the cautious maneuver, he gestured toward the overstuffed chairs grouped in front of the fireplace. "Would you like to sit?"

"No, thank you, I want to know what's going on." She took a deep breath, trying to calm her frayed nerves. *Is all this mystery necessary?*

"Captain Tom Deverane, Sectors Special Forces." He walked to the chairs himself. To be polite, she joined him, shaking his proffered hand before seating herself. "Excuse my dust," he said. "But I've been in the Western Plains and the Abujan mountain range for quite some time now."

"Why don't you try telling me something relevant about why you're here?" Many a slow-moving clerk at the Loxton offices had jumped at that peremptory tone from her.

"I forget you've been out of the loop." Sitting down, Deverane leaned forward, putting his hands on his knees and taking a deep breath. "Two days ago I got urgent orders, relayed from Sector Command, diverting me from my primary mission. The new priority was to come five hundred miles out of our way to extract you for a safe return to the capital city." From the dry tone in his voice, Andi guessed how little he'd appreciated the change. "Now, if you could get your things together, I'd like to be on our way before dark."

She blinked. *Today? He wants me to leave now?* Andi shifted back into the chair's embrace, crossing her legs. "Get my things—what are you talking about? I'm the guest of Lord Tonkiln's family, and I'm expected to present a significant gift from Loxton at the reception tonight with due ceremony. I can't ride off with you on literally a moment's notice without some compelling reason. Why is your Command issuing orders concerning me anyway?"

The captain got up in one smooth motion, like a great cat uncurling, paced to the fireplace and back, then half sat on the edge of a sturdy table. *I bet he's a person in constant motion—discussing anything in patient detail doesn't appear to be his style. Well, I'm not one of his soldiers and I don't take orders from him, so he'd better explain himself.*

"Miss Markriss—"

"Call me Andi." *And let's get this discussion on a less military, more personal level so you stop trying to give me orders.*

The quick, meaningless smile crossed his handsome face again, never reaching his eyes. "*Andi.* In case you haven't heard, this entire planet is about to be embroiled in a devastating Clan war."

Click to get more info about *Escape from Zulaire.*

***

Thanks again for reading STAR SURVIVORS. I really hope you enjoyed it.

You've just read the latest book in *The Sectors SF Romance Series.* All books in this series take place in the same adventurous world of brave space soldiers and the competent ladies who love them. You can read the books back to back, or as individual, stand-alone stories. The other books in the series are *Escape from Zulaire, Wreck of the Nebula Dream, Mission to Mahjundar, Hostage to the Stars,* and *Trapped on Talonque.*

If you'd like to stay up to date on all my new releases, please sign up for my newsletter.

ALSO BY VERONICA SCOTT

Science Fiction Romance
The Star Cruise Series
Star Cruise: Marooned
Star Cruise: Outbreak
Standalone SFR
Lady of the Star Wind

***

Ancient Egyptian Romance
(with a dash of the paranormal too!)

The Gods of Egypt Series
Priestess of the Nile
Warrior of the Nile
Dancer of the Nile
Magic of the Nile
Ghost of the Nile
Healer of the Nile